SUCCEED TO INSPIRE LIKE THE TATAS

Rajiv Agarwal is a family business consultant with more than twenty years of experience. Considered a leading expert on family business in India, he has advised more than 1,500 families on succession, strategy and continuity. Currently a professor of Family Business, Strategy and Entrepreneurship at SP Jain Institute of Management & Research (SPJIMR), Mumbai, which is also his alma mater, Agarwal got his PhD from BITS Pilani and is an alumnus of Harvard Business School. He has been the visiting professor at IIM Kozhikode and IIM Indore, and expert advisor on the Board of Academics, Department of Management, Nirma University, Ahmedabad. He also writes in various publications on topics related to family business.

Also by the same author

Think, Lead & Strategize Like Kumar Mangalam Birla
Lead with Purpose like Anand Mahindra

SUCCEED TO INSPIRE LIKE THE TATAS

RAJIV AGARWAL

Published by
Rupa Publications India Pvt. Ltd 2019
7/16, Ansari Road, Daryaganj
New Delhi 110002

Sales centres:
Allahabad Bengaluru Chennai
Hyderabad Jaipur Kathmandu
Kolkata Mumbai

Copyright © Rajiv Agarwal 2019

The views and opinions expressed in this book are the author's own and
the facts are as reported by him which have been
verified to the extent possible, and the publishers are not in
any way liable for the same.

All rights reserved.

No part of this publication may be reproduced, transmitted,
or stored in a retrieval system, in any form or by any means,
electronic, mechanical, photocopying, recording or otherwise,
without the prior permission of the publisher.

ISBN: 978-93-5333-570-0

First impression 2019

10 9 8 7 6 5 4 3 2 1

The moral right of the author has been asserted.

Printed at HT Media Ltd, Gr. Noida

This book is sold subject to the condition that it shall not,
by way of trade or otherwise, be lent, resold, hired out, or otherwise
circulated, without the publisher's prior consent, in any form of binding or
cover other than that in which it is published.

CONTENTS

Preface		*vii*
The Tata Group: Then & Now		*ix*
The People Behind the Tata Group		*xiii*

1. Embrace Change as the Times Change — 1
2. Align with a Unique Brand Identity: How to Carve One — 9
3. Grow in the Right Spirit: Doing the Right Things like the Tatas — 17
4. Treat Patience as a Virtue — 24
5. Choose Your Industries Strategically — 30
6. Build Trust In Your Business To Grow Your Business — 37
7. Face Adversity Head-on: The Tata-DoCoMo Saga — 43
8. Growth by Acquisition: The Tata's Takeover Strategy — 50
9. Discard Rigid Management Styles: How to Develop Environmental Flexibility — 84
10. Humility is Imperative for Business Success — 91

11. Taking Over in Style:
    The J.R.D.-Ratan Tata Dynamics 96
12. Tread the Untrodden Path:
    The Tatas & Nation-Building 108
13. Choose Your Priorities Wisely:
    Positive Social Impact vs Profit 116
14. Adopt Global Standards from the Outset 133
15. To Experience Success, First Envision It Clearly 144
16. The Tata Nano: Mega Lessons from the Small Car 152
17. Exiting is Not Failure 160
18. Summing Up: Management Lessons
    For Your Business 164

Annexure 1 170
Annexure 2 172
Annexure 3 173

PREFACE

The Tatas are an institution, and not just an illustrious family whose immense contribution to nation-building helped lay down the foundation of modern-day India. Penning down this book has been a humbling journey for me. I believe that one cannot do justice—in such a compact book—to the achievements of the Group over time, many of which have been the springboard for economic and social development in the country.

This book studies the Tata Group with the intention of bringing forth valuable management lessons for business leaders, entrepreneurs and students. In writing this book, I have carefully handpicked those instances from the workings of the Tata Group that I thought to be the most educational. In selectively addressing a few issues from a wide gamut of subjects, I have assumed certain creative liberties. There are, of course, several subjects I haven't been able to touch upon for various reasons. Readers would be advised not to treat this book as a comprehensive and conclusive record of the achievements of the Tata Group but the subjective interpretation of one author designed specifically for use in an educational environment.

Additionally, since the sources for all the materials in this book are published media sources, there are possibilities of this book suffering inaccuracies due to this reason. Readers are advised to keep this in mind while reading this book.

Hence, in this context, I have attempted to consolidate some of the vital management lessons from the Tata Group—lessons that I consider as the tip of the proverbial iceberg. I hope this book will serve as a primer to understand the workings of a business empire that has established itself as the forerunner of positive change. Having said that, I also realize that the Tata's journey yet has a long way to go.

THE TATA GROUP: THEN & NOW

The business history of the Tata Group is deeply interconnected with the economic progress of India. The contributions of the Tatas have played an invaluable role in determining the economic, intellectual and social development of our nation. The Group operates under a mission that is a unique blend of the strategic and the philanthropic. Their website quotes their mission as:

> To improve the quality of life of the communities we serve globally, through long-term stakeholder value creation based on Leadership with Trust.[1]

As of 2019, the Tata Group comprises thirty companies with a presence in more than hundred countries across six continents. The ten verticals are Information Technology (IT), Automotive, Steel, Consumer and Retail, Infrastructure, Aerospace and Defence, Financial Services, Tourism and Travel, Telecom and Media, and Trading and Investments. Several

---

[1]Corporate website, www.tata.com, accessed 9 March 2019

of the Group companies are renowned in both business and community circles. Some of them include Tata Consultancy Services (TCS), Tata Motors, Tata Steel, Tata Chemicals, Tata Global Beverages, Titan, Tata Capital, Tata Power, Tata Advanced Systems, Indian Hotels Company Limited (IHCL) and Tata Communications.

The companies in the Tata Group are promoted by Tata Sons, the holding company. However, they operate with complete independence; each one has its own supervisory Board of directors. In 2017–18, the Tata Group earned a total revenue of $110.7 billion, employing over 700,000 people. At that time (as of 31 March 2018), the market capitalization of twenty-eight of the listed Tata companies was approximately $145.3 billion.[2]

WELFARE ACTIVITIES: THE TATA TRUSTS STRUCTURE

Over successive generations, the Tata family has bequeathed much of its personal wealth to numerous philanthropic Trusts. Seven Trusts together form the Tata Trusts, namely, 1) Sir Dorabji Tata Trust and the Allied Trusts (SDTT), 2) Sir Ratan Tata Trust (SRTT), 3) J.R.D. Tata Trust, 4) R.D. Tata Trust, 5) Tata Education Trust, 6) Tata Social Welfare Trust and 7) Sarvajanik Seva Trust.

Today, these philanthropic arms—primarily Sir Dorabji Tata Trust and Sir Ratan Tata Trust—control a significant portion (66 per cent) of the shares of Tata Sons, the Group's

---

[2]Tata corporate website, https://www.tata.com/investors, accessed 10 May 2019

holding company. This shareholding structure is unique in India's business environment, wherein as much as two-thirds of the total equity capital is held by philanthropic Trusts.

In turn, these Trusts are engaged in various welfare activities for the upliftment of the country. They support an impressive assortment of causes, from education to healthcare.

The Tata Group, as a business empire, has been the pioneer in providing numerous benefits for employees, some of which were rolled out in India much before they were initiated elsewhere. In 1912, Tata Steel introduced eight-hour working days—a marked improvement from the previous standard of twelve hours. In 1920, the Group started a provident fund scheme for its employees; the Government of India introduced it much later in 1952. The Group is also renowned for setting up townships with extensive facilities for the employees.

As a business empire, the Tata Group has consistently shown a keen dedication to philanthropy. This commitment emanates from a well-rounded business perspective that prioritizes the welfare of those integral to business: shareholders and employees. Mr Jamsetji Tata, Group Founder, famously said:

> We do not claim to be more unselfish, more generous or more philanthropic than other people. But we think we started on sound and straightforward business principles, considering the interests of the shareholders our own, and the health and welfare of the employees, the sure foundation of our success.[3]

---

[3] Corporate website, https://www.tatachemicals.com/ebook/tcoc/files/basic-html/page3.html, accessed 9 May 2019

A Section of the Tata Family Tree

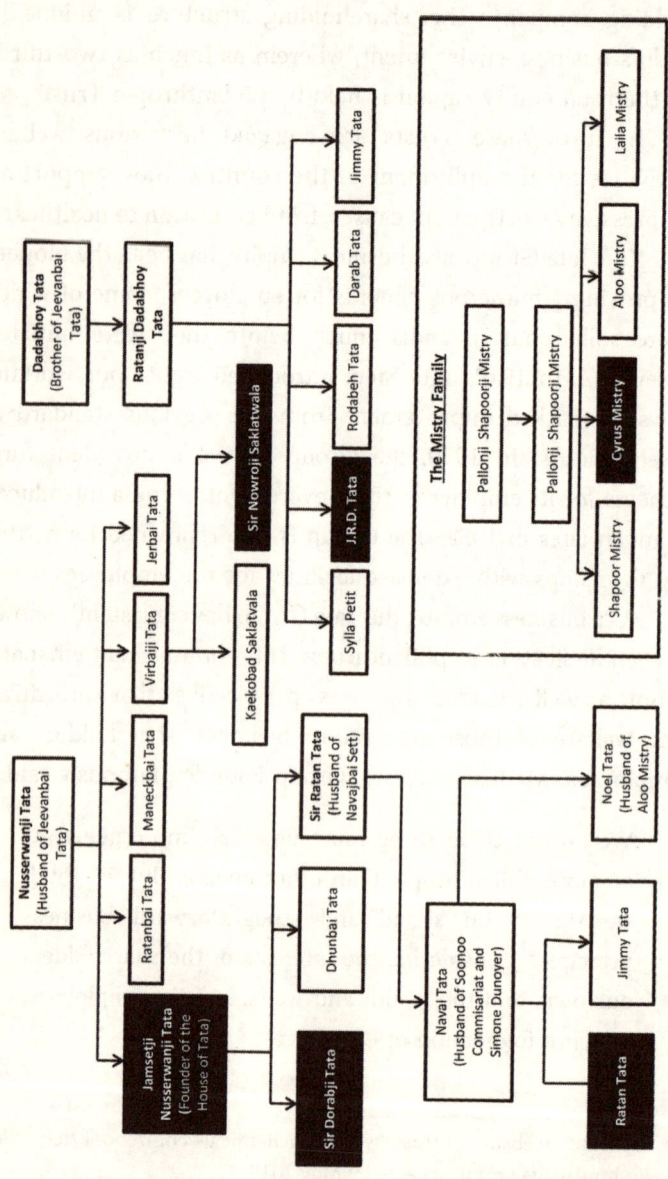

Source: Compiled by the author from various sources

THE PEOPLE BEHIND THE TATA GROUP

The origins of the Tata Group can be traced back to the birth of Mr Jamsetji Nusserwanji Tata in 1839, in Navsari, Gujarat. He was born in a family of Parsi Zoroastrian priests. His father, Mr Nusserwanji Tata, had been the first businessman in the family—a step that broke away from tradition and was promptly followed by his son.

JAMSETJI NUSSERWANJI TATA

The groundwork for the Tata Group was really laid in 1868, when, at the age of twenty-nine, Mr Jamsetji Tata started a trading company. He had a starting capital of ₹21,000. Mr Jamsetji Tata had then recently returned from a trip to England where he had learnt about the textile business. He returned to India convinced of the tremendous potential in the textile business. In 1869, he acquired a bankrupt mill and got to work in turning its fortunes around. In 1871, he sold this once-beleaguered mill as a transformed business entity called Alexandra Mill.

From then on, Mr Jamsetji Tata started floating new companies with an infectious mix of enthusiasm and strategy. In 1874, he started a company called Central India Spinning, Weaving and Manufacturing Company Limited. Subsequently, in 1877, he started the Empress Mills. He also envisioned setting up an iron and steel company that would generate hydroelectricity as well as a world-class educational institution to further scientific temperament in the country. Eventually, these dreams were realized by his successors, in the form of Tata Iron and Steel Company (TISCO) in Jamshedpur, Tata Power in Mumbai and the Indian Institute of Science (IISc) in Bengaluru.

Mr Jamsetji Tata, the founder of the Tata Group, served as its chairman from 1868 to 1904. During his tenure, he approached new ventures with an astute vision. In 1902, while planning the steel plant township in Jamshedpur, he explained the concept in a letter to his son:

> Be sure to lay wide streets planted with shady trees, every other of a quick-growing variety. Be sure that there is plenty of space for lawns and gardens. Reserve large areas for football, hockey and parks. Earmark areas for Hindu temples, Mohammedan mosques and Christian churches.[1]

The above guidelines were outlined and shared five years before even a site had been decided!

---

[1] Corporate website, http://www.tata.com/aboutus/articlesinside/The-giant-who-touched-tomorrow, accessed 9 March 2019

FROM JAMSETJI TO SIR DORABJI

In 1904, after Jamsetji Tata's death in Germany, the chairmanship of the Tata Group passed on to his elder son, Sir Dorabji Tata. One of his first initiatives after assuming the chairmanship was completing his father's dream projects: setting up the TISCO in 1907 and kick-starting hydroelectric power generation with Tata Power in 1915 (near Mumbai, then Bombay).

Sir Dorabji Tata was a firm believer in using one's acquired wealth for constructive purposes. In less than a year after his wife Meherbai's death, he donated all his wealth to the Sir Dorabji Tata Trust, insisting that it must be used 'without any distinction of place, nationality or creed', for the advancement of learning and research, relief of distress, and other charitable purposes. He died three months after bequeathing all his wealth to charity.

The wealth that Sir Dorabji Tata turned over to the Trust comprised substantial shareholdings in Tata Sons, Indian Hotels and allied companies; land and other property; and twenty-one pieces of jewellery left by his wife, including the famous Jubilee Diamond. The diamond was then estimated to be valued at ₹10 million. As of 2019, the valuation of the entire wealth donated by Sir Dorabji Tata would be worth more than ₹500 million.

SIR NOWROJI SAKLATWALA

In 1932, after Sir Dorabji Tata's death, the chairmanship of the Group was transferred to Sir Nowroji Saklatwala, Jamsetji

Tata's nephew. He assumed the reins at the helm, serving as the third chairman of the Group for six years until his demise in 1938 in France.

At the time, the Tata Group had ventured into various new areas, including insurance and the production of soaps, detergents and cooking oil. As Mr R.M. Lala said in *Beyond the Last Blue Mountain*, a book chronicling the life of the Tatas, 'Sir Nowroji's job was to hold on to what the Tatas had, and this he did well.'[2]

THE J.R.D. TATA ERA

On 26 July 1938, the Board of Tata Sons met after Sir Nowroji died of a heart attack in Europe. At this meeting, Jehangir Ratanji Dadabhoy Tata (J.R.D. Tata) was appointed as the new chairman of the Tata Group. He was the son of Mr R.D. Tata, a business partner and relative of Mr Jamsetji Tata. At the time of assuming his new role, J.R.D. was only thirty-four years old.

Mr J.R.D. Tata's association with the Tata Group has deep-seated origins. He had joined the business empire in 1925 as an unpaid apprentice. Since 1926, after the death of his father, he had served on the Board of Tata Sons.

When Mr J.R.D. Tata became the Group chairman, one of his first moves was the setting up of Tata Aviation Service in 1932. His childhood passion for flying had undoubtedly influenced this gigantic business move. Tata Aviation Service was to be the precursor to Tata Airlines and Air India, India's

---

[2] R.M. Lala, *Beyond the Last Blue Mountain: A life of J.R.D. Tata*, Penguin Random House India, 2017, Page 76

national carrier. When the first flight in the history of Indian aviation took off (from Drigh Road in Karachi, Pakistan to Mumbai), Mr J.R.D. Tata was at the controls of the airplane. It was a pivotal moment that would determine the face of Indian aviation in the years to come.

In 1953, the Indian government nationalized Air India. Even after the nationalization, Mr J.R.D. Tata stayed at the helm as the chairman until 1977.

During the fifty-odd years that Mr J.R.D. Tata was the chairman, the Tata Group expanded into various new areas of business. These included choices that would reap rich dividends in the future: Tata Chemicals (1939), Tata Motors (1945), Tata Industries (1945), Voltas (1954), Tata Tea (1964), TCS (1968) and Titan Watches Limited (later renamed to Titan Company Limited) (1984).

Under Mr J.R.D. Tata's leadership, the Group grew in spite of tightening government controls. He consistently encouraged professionals to run the independent businesses, steadily turning the Group into a conglomerate. This move was well-thought-out: it promoted both entrepreneurial talent and expertise. There was a flipside to it though: it also gave rise to fiefdoms, thereby effectively reducing the corporate office control over the various companies. Mr J.R.D. Tata endeavoured to rein the companies in, once he assessed that this situation could become perilous, but these efforts were in vain.

The 1990s brought about a massive change: the opening up of the Indian economy. The Tata Group was a traditional conservative business conglomerate.[3] Their perception, in the market, even today, is that the Group was too diverse, spread too thinly across too many areas in too many industries.[4] The businesses operated primarily in commodity sectors in protected markets where traditional practices worked just fine. Also, the Tata Group held small stakes in many of its companies—a situation that exposed it to the risk of takeovers.[5] After the economic reforms were unfurled in 1991, the increased competition would necessitate changes in the way the Group operated.

Mr J.R.D. Tata passed away on 29 November 1993, a couple of years after Mr Ratan Tata had assumed the role of the next chairman.

RATAN TATA

When Mr Ratan Tata took over as the chairman in 1991, the Tata Group had a turnover of ₹8,000 crore. When Mr Ratan Tata stepped down in 2012, the Group had a turnover of

---

[3]PTI, 'We changed our "conservative" ways after economic reforms in 1991: Ratan Tata', *The Times of India*, 4 March 2012, accessed 10 May 2019, https://timesofindia.indiatimes.com/business/india-business/We-changed-our-conservative-ways-after-economic-reforms-in-1991-Ratan-Tata/articleshow/12135103.cms

[4]Simon Mundy and Victor Mallet, 'Tata Boss: "I needed to stop the bleeding"', *Financial Times*, 19 February 2018, accessed 10 May 2019, https://www.ft.com/content/b2c39d0c-1194-11e8-940e-08320fc2a277

[5]Reeba Zachariah, 'Tata Sons to acquire group entities' shares', *The Times of India*, 13 September 2017, accessed 11 May 2019, https://timesofindia.indiatimes.com/business/india-business/tata-sons-to-acquire-group-entities-shares/articleshow/60486865.cms

₹4,75,721 crore![6] By 2015, the Group acquired twenty-two companies globally at a total cost of $15 billion. In 2019, the Group has operations in over hundred countries across six continents and exports to over 120 nations. Almost 6,60,800 employees are a part of the Group today.

Clearly, the kind of success that the empire has witnessed under the leadership of Mr Ratan Tata has been phenomenal. This achievement is even more remarkable, when seen in the light of the changed realities that Mr Ratan Tata had to deal with, and the TATA Group's response to these threats, notably increased competition and revised rules for conducting business in India.

After commencing his tenure as the chairman, Mr Ratan Tata started consolidating the Group. He ensured central office control of an empire that had hitherto been operating under individual fiefdoms. Previously, charismatic leaders such as Russi Mody at Tata Steel Ltd and Darbari Seth at Tata Chemicals Ltd had assumed almost unchecked powers in their corresponding companies. But their powers were now curtailed and soon, they were eased out.[7]

In 2006–07, Mr Ratan Tata bought Corus Group plc, a UK-based steelmaker, for $12 billion. This decision steered the Group to the position of one of the largest steelmakers in the

---

[6]PTI, 'Ratan Tata retires as Tata Group chairman', *Business Today*, 28 January 2013, accessed 24 May 2019, https://www.businesstoday.in/current/corporate/ratan-tata-retires-as-tata-group-chairman/story/191096.html

[7]Sundeep Khanna, 'Uneasy lies the Tata crown', LiveMint, 26 October 2016, accessed 9 May 2019, http://www.livemint.com/Opinion/GzoFRxvCVQXC6I gxI54FVN/Uneasy-lies-the-Tata-crown.html

world. (Unfortunately, as explained in a later chapter, it also led to huge losses in later years, brought on by adverse turns in the commodity cycle, when the prices globally dipped, thus causing revenues and hence profits to decline.)

With Mr Ratan Tata at the helm, the Group undertook diversification in a substantial manner. In 1996, he set up Tata Teleservices to explore India's expanding telecom market. This was followed by the acquisition of 45 per cent stake in Videsh Sanchar Nigam Limited (VSNL) in 2002 (it acquired the balance stake in 2008, and renamed it from VSNL to Tata Communications). VSNL was then India's top international telecom service provider. In 2004, TCS went public in what was the largest initial public offering (IPO) in the private sector in the Indian stock market until then. The Group also extensively explored alternatives in the automobile sector. While 1998 saw the launch of the Indica (India's first indigenously made car), 2008 witnessed the unveiling of the Tata Nano (more popularly known as the ₹1-lakh car). Mr Ratan Tata also undertook other far-sighted moves for the Group's consolidation, significant among which were the takeover of Tetley, a large tea company in the UK, in 2000 and the sale of the Group's stakes in Tata Oil Mills (1993) and ACC (starting in 1999), a leading cement company in India.

Mr Ratan Tata's strategy for the growth of the Tata Group was one that envisioned a leadership position in the Indian market as well as a force to be reckoned with in the global business world. He summed it up as follows:

> One hundred years from now, I expect the Tatas to be much bigger, of course, than it is now. More importantly,

> I hope the group comes to be regarded as being the best in India—best in the manner in which we operate, best in the products we deliver, and best in our value system and ethics.
>
> Having said that, I hope that a hundred years from now we will spread our wings far beyond India, that we become a global group, operating in many countries, an Indian business conglomerate that is at home in the world, carrying the same sense of trust that we do today.

In line with this strategy, Mr Ratan Tata also invested his energies in the acquisitions of foreign enterprises to establish the Group's global presence. In 2000, Tata Tea acquired Tetley. Soon after, in 2004, Tata Motors acquired the heavy vehicles unit of Daewoo Motors, South Korea. In 2004, Tata Steel acquired NatSteel, the Singapore-based steel company, while Tata Chemicals secured a controlling stake in the UK-based Brunner Mond Group Ltd, a chemical manufacturing company. The acquisitions continued in 2007 when Tata Steel acquired Corus, the Anglo-Dutch giant. In 2008, Tata Motors acquired the Jaguar and Land Rover brands of the Ford Motor Company. Throughout these dynamic times, Mr Ratan Tata endeavoured to retain, as well as strengthen, the Group's ethical stand, unwilling to let global expansion interfere with long-held, core Indian values.

CYRUS MISTRY

In November 2011, Mr Cyrus Mistry was announced the handpicked successor of Mr Ratan Tata. He was to shadow

Mr Ratan Tata for a year, before assuming the position of the chairman in December 2012. The decision to choose Mr Mistry as the Group chairman was a conscious move to further the professionalism of a business empire that had previously only been steered by family insiders.

However, Mr Mistry's tenure as the chairman was short, lasting only from 2012 to 2016. In October 2016, the Tata Sons Board withdrew support for Mr Cyrus Mistry and removed him as the chairman. Various events led to his stepping down, the most publicly discussed of which was the Board's lack of confidence in Mr Mistry's leadership. Mr Ratan Tata briefly replaced him until January 2017, when Mr Natarajan Chandrasekaran, the Managing Director and CEO of TCS, was appointed as the chairman. Since then, Mr Chandrasekaran had taken several steps (such as settling the DoCoMo case, or trying to merge the Tata Steel European business, or considering divestments) to steer the Tata Group to keep it relevant for the future and to improve the profitability of the Group.

Over the years, the Tata Group has grown phenomenally by employing an interesting mix of business strategies. While it has focused on reviving existing businesses, it has also forayed into new areas and foreign markets. Alongside, the Group has manufactured innovative products and worked on creating a distinctive brand identity.

Going forward, the Tata's approach to business in an ever-changing world is explained clearly on their website:

> The Tata group is now more cohesive and united than it has ever been. This is no accident; rather, it is the

outcome of a set of policies that have been emphasised and reinforced by former Chairman Ratan Tata and the Group Corporate Centre, the top decision-making body in the Group. There's more to the new-world Tata.

The pursuit of business excellence has become the norm and there is a focus on innovation. What have not changed are the group's emphasis on ethical business practices and its commitment to the communities in which it operates.[8]

---

[8]Corporate website, www.tata.com, accessed 9 November 2016

1
EMBRACE CHANGE
AS THE TIMES CHANGE

BE DETERMINED IN THE PURSUIT OF SUCCESS FOR YOUR BUSINESS, BUT DON'T HOLD ON TO OLD PRACTICES THAT HAVE LOST THEIR UTILITY.

The Tatas have shown remarkable foresight in realizing what works for the business and, when needed, have changed themselves to be in sync with the requirements of the times. While the Tata Group does have deep roots and a firm foundation steeped in traditional values, it does not believe in maintaining old practices if they are found to be inadequate.

REFORMING MANAGEMENT STYLES

When Mr J.R.D. Tata became the Group chairman, he made a significant change in the management style followed within the company. He recalled that Sir Nowroji Saklatwala, his predecessor, would rush from one Board meeting to another throughout his six years as the chairman. This did not leave him with enough time for creative or original thought. This seemed like an unacceptable situation to Mr J.R.D. Tata.

Traditionally, the chairman of Tata Sons, the holding company, would also be the chairman of the Tata companies. Mr J.R.D. Tata decided to break free from this long-held tradition. His focus was on spreading the empire's wings to newer industries, and this could happen only when he, as the Group chairman, had the time and energy to think about new ventures. He handed over the chairmanship of some of the Group companies to experienced people within the Group, while retaining a few positions that he adjudged crucial, for himself. For instance, he remained actively involved with Tata Sons, Tata Steel and Tata Airlines. This decentralization in management was a significant change in tune with the need of the hour—growth by expansion.

The Tata Group witnessed yet another change in management style when Mr Ratan Tata took over from Mr J.R.D. Tata. One of his first realizations after assuming office was the need to regain control over the Group companies, which had started operating as successful but individually operating fiefdoms. He initiated this control by returning the control of operations to a centralized entity—the Group chairman's office.

Mr Ratan Tata's reversal of Mr J.R.D. Tata's managerial decisions might come across as time-consuming. What good did the former change do if it had to be undone? But here it is essential to note that the managerial decisions were in tandem with the times. Mr Ratan Tata's management style was based on the realization that the Group would have to function in a more cohesive manner if the vision was to be realized. It wouldn't do to have the different arms working independently. It was a step attuned to the newer environment that was a far cry from the business environment in which Mr J.R.D. Tata had operated.

Along with restoring centralized control over the Group, Mr Ratan Tata also championed the divesting of companies that were not central to its core. But he ensured that this was done with utmost sensitivity for the workforce. For instance, while divesting Tata Oil Mills Company (TOMCO), an agreement was drawn to protect the jobs of the 5,500 employees, distributors and suppliers for three years.[1]

Mr Cyrus Mistry's tenure of nearly four years was probably too short to arrive at any assessment, but he did make some decisions following a strategy of divesting assets, keeping in mind the long-term interests of the Tata Group.[2] Mr Cyrus Mistry alleged serious governance issues with his dismissal and sued the Tatas, but all these allegations were denied by them.[3]

---

[1] Shashank Shah, *The Tata Group: From Torchbearers to Trailblazers*, Penguin Random House India, 2018, page 36

[2] PTI, 'Cyrus Mistry's Tata journey: From Surprise entry to unexpected exit', LiveMint, 24 October 2016, accessed 25 May 2019, https://www.livemint.com/Companies/Y0sLSXtiWDGnEz6f93qa7I/Cyrus-Mistrys-Tata-journey-From-surprise-entry-to-unexpec.html

[3] Simon Mundy and Victor Mallet, 'Tata Boss: "I needed to stop the bleeding"', *Financial Times*, 19 February 2018, accessed 10 May 2019, https://www.

The next chairman, Mr N. Chandrasekaran had a single priority, to stop the bleeding[4], that is, make the businesses more profitable and more efficient. He took steps such as replacing some heads in key operating companies, where he felt that the right people were not leading those companies. He also settled the dispute with Japanese company NTT DoCoMo, and merged Tata Steel's European plant with Germany's ThyssenKrupp. He is examining each business to decide whether to scale it up, merge it with other Group companies to remove duplication or sell it.[5] In May 2019, he merged all the branded food businesses from Tata Chemicals Ltd into Tata Global Beverages, and renamed it to Tata Consumer Products.[6]

TOUGH DECISIONS IN THE FACE OF COMPETITION: THE TBEM AWARDS

During his chairmanship, Mr Ratan Tata instituted the JRD QV Award in 1994. This award was based on a similar process as the Malcolm Baldrige National Quality Award (MBNQA), the renowned global quality award that recognizes multi-sector organizations for performance excellence. It was licenced by the Tatas and modified to be used as an internal award for

---

ft.com/content/b2c39d0c-1194-11e8-940e-08320fc2a277
[4]Ibid.
[5]Ibid.
[6]Kalpana Pathak and Prasannata Patwa, 'Tata puts its food business on a single platter', LiveMint, 16 May 2019, accessed 25 May 2019, https://www.livemint.com/companies/news/tata-chemicals-consumer-business-merged-with-tata-global-1557917946150.html

the Group companies. Eventually, it was renamed as the Tata Business Excellence Model (TBEM).[7]

In the award's first year, some of the top twelve Tata companies were selected for the application. The selected companies were audited under the TBEM award process. The results of the audit (of the shortlisted twelve Tata companies), however, disappointed Mr Ratan Tata. They showed that these twelve companies had scored an average of only 215 out of 1,000 possible points.[8] Mr Ratan Tata believed that an acceptable score should be no less than 600 points.

The senior leaders were also concerned at the outcome; they realized it was time to reflect and raise some difficult questions. A series of meetings to get to the root of the problem revealed a possible clue. The management of the chosen companies was manufacturing-oriented. So, the companies focused primarily on expanding the production, achieving the set production targets and increasing profits every year. That sounded fine in theory—what could be its undoing?

Well, the manufacturing-focused approach worked fine in the era of production efficiencies and the controlled production era—the Licence Raj—where one could (potentially) sell whatever one produced. But the world had changed. The liberalization policies introduced by the Indian government had ushered in multiple players vying for greater

---

[7] https://www.tatabex.com/about-us/tata-business-excellence-model, accessed 6 April 2019

[8] Shashank Shah, *The Tata Group: From Torchbearers to Trailblazers*, Penguin Random House India, 2018, Kindle edition, Location 922 of 8284

market share. In this customer-focused era where competition was perpetually on the upswing, the manufacturing-focused approach had serious flaws. It was no longer sufficient to be a large domestic producer, but one had to be globally competitive, which was a prerequisite of success.

Mr Ratan Tata surmised that there was only one solution to the problem: the Group companies had to start paying attention to the new-age, discerning customer. It was a task that could be accomplished only if the quality improved at the process level itself.

However, it seemed that Mr Ratan Tata's sentiments were not shared by the top management of the Group companies. For the next six years from 1995, none of the companies was able to win the award. In fact, bagging the award did not seem to appear in the list of priorities for these companies.

Mr Rata Tata decided it was time to make a tough call. In a subsequent meeting with the CEOs of the Group companies, he raised the issue of his dissatisfaction with the low scores in the TBEM audits. He questioned the inability of any company to win the award, expressing disappointment that not a single company had performed as per his expectations. But it did not stop there. Mr Ratan Tata issued an ultimatum to ensure that the management would start taking the issue seriously and not brush it under the carpet. Mr Ratan Tata announced at the meeting that the following year he would not like to see any CEO who was unwilling to follow the stated guidelines and use the TBEM to drive business excellence. It was, simply put, perform or perish.

Eventually, the TBEM award *did* help the Tata companies

work towards achieving business excellence. The TBEM had criteria which helped the Tata companies focus on key areas such as market, customer and processes, continuous improvement and employees.

The TBEM was upgraded every two years, with the Group introducing new elements in the evaluation criteria. For example, in 2005, the weightages to various items were modified, and four areas of emphasis were identified, viz. climate change, safety, innovation and corporate governance. In 2008, safety processes and safety experts were introduced.[9] Other topics which were introduced included Knowledge Management (in 2003), Sustainability and Climate Change (in 2005–07), Technology and Digitization (in 2011–12) and Customer Promise (in 2015).

By 2016, the award covered business dimensions such as Leadership, Strategy, Customer and Market Focus, Measurement Analysis, Knowledge Management, Workforce Focus, Operations and Business Results.[10]

TAKEAWAY

The Tata Group has been in business for almost 152 years—over fifteen decades. It has long been associated with having

---

[9] *The Business Times Singapore*, 'Tata Adapts own Business Excellence Model', 23 October 2014, ASQ.com, accessed 10 May 2019, http://asq.org/qualitynews/qnt/execute/displaySetup?newsID=19277

[10] Press Trust of India, 'Tata Steel recognised as Industry Leader under TBEM assessment', *Business Standard*, 29 July 2016, accessed 10 May 2019, https://www.business-standard.com/article/pti-stories/tata-steel-recognised-as-industry-leader-under-tbem-assessment-116072901613_1.html

a firm foundation of traditions and established practices. But be that as it may, the Group has shown immense foresight in embracing change. The leadership has made conscious efforts to bring in changes in the business whenever required, including modifications in the management style, quality control and process-level improvement. It is this ability to welcome—and actually encourage—change that has been a key factor in the Group's continued success even in transforming times.

In the context of the TBEM awards, the Group proved its level of commitment to this change-driven business philosophy. The people at the helm were willing to make tough calls, if needed, but not give in to complacency. Mr Ratan Tata's stern—and, in all probability, unpopular—stand shows his determination to get the CEOs aligned with his vision for the business empire. He displayed the willingness to take a call that he deemed necessary to direct the Group in the right direction.

Indeed, business leaders cannot always play it safe; in fact, they rarely can. Certain business decisions may not go down well with the Board or the employees, but these tough unpleasant decisions have to be made for the long-term success of the organization. It is worthwhile doing this, if it means cementing the path towards sustainable business growth.

2
ALIGN WITH A UNIQUE BRAND IDENTITY: HOW TO CARVE ONE

CREATE A COMMON BRAND IDENTITY FOR YOUR BUSINESS TO FURTHER UNIFICATION, UNLEASHING SYNERGIES AND CONSOLIDATION OF CONTROL.

> *The intention has been to create a single strong entity that will benefit all (Tata) companies... If you are to fight a Mitsubishi or an X or Y in the free India of tomorrow, you better have one rather than 40 brands. You better have the ability to promote that brand in a meaningful manner...*
> —Mr Ratan Tata in an interview to
> *The Economic Times* in 1996[11]

---

[11]'Brand Name to Survive Personalities: Ratan', *The Economic Times*, 14 October 1996 quoted in: Tarun Khanna, Krishna Palepu and Danielle Melito Wu, 'House of Tata, 1995: The Next Generation (A)', HBS Case

When Mr Ratan Tata took over as the chairman of the Tata Group, he perceived one significant challenge: a lack of consistency in the Tata brand. He found that the various Tata companies failed to use the parent brand consistently; there were several differences in the way the brand was presented to the public by the Tata companies (that is, there was no consistency in the way the brand, the logo or the colours were used, with different companies using them differently). Mr Ratan Tata figured that if the Group were to use its brand perception favourably to counter competition, it would first have to make things consistent. It was possible, he surmised, to use the Tata brand to align the different interests of the Group and present one cohesive, identifiable front. How could he go about achieving this?

Mr Ratan Tata figured that he would need to undertake three concrete steps:

1. Clarify the definition of the brand
2. Establish the ownership of the brand
3. Decide how it could and should be used

All the above would have to be accomplished in a manner that could be institutionalized across the Group.

In 1998, Mr Ratan Tata established the Brand Equity and Business Promotion (BEBP) agreement. This agreement had to be accepted by all the Tata-promoted companies. The following were the terms:

1. A uniform brand logo would be used across all Tata

companies. A new logo was designed—a white 'T' inside a light-blue oval. The Tata name was also redesigned to lend it a more modern look.
2. All the companies would adopt the Tata Code of Conduct (TCC) and the TBEM (see Chapter 1).
3. All the companies that used the Tata name directly or had a strong association with it would have to pay a fee of 0.25 per cent of their turnover (but not more than 5 per cent of their profits before tax). The companies that did not use the brand name would have to pay a fee of 0.15 per cent.[12] While the others would have to pay 0.10 per cent. Joint venture partners where the foreign partner was offering their brand name free would not pay any fee.[13] The amount collected would be used for the development, promotion and protection of the Tata brand.

The BEBP agreement met with a lot of resistance, especially from the top executives of some of the prominent Group companies. They felt that they had not used the Tata name to further their companies' interests and hence, did not need to pay the stated fee. However, Mr Ratan Tata defended the terms vehemently. He stood up in favour of the royalty fees as

---

[12]Morgen Witzel, *Tata: The Evolution of a Corporate Brand*, Penguin India, 2012, page 65; Sharad Sarin, *Strategic Brand Management for B2B Markets: A Road Map for Organizational Transformation*, Response Books India, 2010, page 78

[13]Charubala Annuncio, 'Tata's Brand Royalties', *Outlook*, 30 October 1996, accessed 11 May 2019, https://www.outlookindia.com/magazine/story/tatas-brand-royalties/202412

well, stating that in its absence, many of the firms were likely to use the Tata name to seek new collaborations or speak to their respective bankers. But they would conveniently forget this important fact once their goal had been achieved.

Eventually, in 1998, seven Tata companies—TISCO, Tata Engineering and Locomotive Company (TELCO), Tata Tea, Tata Chemicals, the Tata Electric Companies, Tata International and Tata Industries—signed the agreement. Their logos were replaced by the common Group logo. TELCO assumed the new name of Tata Motors in 2003 while TISCO was renamed as Tata Steel in 2005.

The creation and establishment of one brand identity led to several positive outcomes for the Group. For starters, the step helped to consolidate the formerly disparate companies under one brand umbrella. Not only did it generate a sense of unity and group identity, but it also aided and unified group communication (both internal and external). The path was now set for improved consolidation within the Group.

The brand-building exercise also showed impressive results in market valuation. In 2015, the value of the Tata brand as determined by Brand Finance, a UK-based consulting firm, increased to $15 billion[14] (₹1,30,000 crore) from ₹3,700 crore in 1997.[15] This was a meteoric rise! In 2019, when the firm

---

[14] P.R. Sanjai, 'At $15 billion, Tata remains India's most valuable brand', LiveMint, https://www.livemint.com/Companies/VPXs8HeCb7jEnZ2 AapzB4H/At-15-billion-Tata-remains-Indias-most-valuable-brand.html, accessed 7 April 2019

[15] Abhineet Kumar, 'Tata Sons' move to cap brand fee is in contrast to its peers', *Business Standard*, 16 July 2015, accessed 7 April 2019, https:// www.business-standard.com/article/economy-policy/tata-sons-move-

performed a subsequent valuation, the Tata brand was still the highest valued in India, with a valuation of $19.5 billion (approximately ₹1,34,550 crore as per 2019 exchange rates).[16]

In fact, the outcome of the BEBP agreement was very successful financially, and over time, the fees collected under it escalated to massive amounts (₹561 crore for 2017–18[17]), in line with increasing revenues. This almost created a quandary for the Group. Let us study it in some detail.

In 2015, a report published in *Business Standard* made a strong case for instating a cap on the royalties being paid by the various Tata companies.[18] This was fuelled by the sky-high royalties being paid by some of the Group companies. For instance, in 2014–15, TCS paid up ₹118 crore. This added a massive chunk to the total collection of Tata Sons that year—a staggering ₹453 crore. Companies like Tata Motors and Tata Steel were also paying steep amounts in fees as per the BEBP agreement. The situation worried some investors,

---

to-cap-brand-fee-is-in-contrast-to-its-peers-115062900916_1.html

[16]Press Trust of India, 'At $19.5 bn, Tata ranks 86th among 100 most valuable global brands: Report', *Business Standard*, 28 January 2019, accessed 11 May 2019, https://www.business-standard.com/article/companies/at-19-5-bn-tata-ranks-86th-among-100-most-valuable-global-brands-report-119012800699_1.html

[17]Rajesh Kurup, 'Tata Sons' debt rises by a billion dollars in FY18', *The Hindu Businessline*, 31 October 2018, accessed 11 May 2019, https://www.thehindubusinessline.com/companies/tata-sons-debt-rises-by-a-billion-dollars-in-fy18/article25373035.ece

[18]Abhineet Kumar, 'Tata Sons' move to cap brand fee is in contrast to its peers', *Business Standard*, 16 July 2015, accessed 7 April 2019, https://www.business-standard.com/article/economy-policy/tata-sons-move-to-cap-brand-fee-is-in-contrast-to-its-peers-115062900916_1.html

and they started raising concerns about the arrangement floated by Mr Ratan Tata. This concern may have arisen from a perception that this could be seen as an alternative way of transferring profits from the profitable companies to Tata Sons.

However, this concern soon proved to be unfounded. The Tata Group clarified that there was *always* a cap. While it had been ₹50 crore until 2012–13, it was raised to ₹75 crore in 2015.[19] This cap was put to reduce the burden on the larger profitable Group companies and to free up cash for growth. (Companies making losses were exempted from paying these royalties). Moreover, the collected funds were being used for building the brand—an exercise that had continuously shown positive results over the period of time. Mr Ratan Tata had pointed out that the biggest gains were accruing to the smaller companies, by associating with the Tata Group and benefitting from the Tata goodwill.[20] It was a win-win situation.

TAKEAWAY

The need for brand-building and carving a unique identity has been seen in most multi-industry groups that may have grown (almost) too fast, with multiple companies in the group.

---

[19]Reeba Zachariah, 'Tata Sons caps group companies' brand fee at Rs75 crore', *The Times of India*, 29 June 2015, accessed 11 May 2019, https://timesofindia.indiatimes.com/business/india-business/Tata-Sons-caps-group-companies-brand-fee-at-Rs-75-crore/articleshow/47858586.cms

[20]Shashank Shah, *The Tata Group: From Torchbearers to Trailblazers*, Penguin Random House India, 2018, Kindle edition, Chapter 4, Location 988 of 8284

There usually comes a stage where the business leader must consolidate the group under one brand umbrella. This also becomes an essential move to build group synergies. It was a step that the Tata Group also took at the time, attempting to unite its operations in multiple industries and make the most of its positive brand perceptions.

An exercise of brand-building has several advantages besides getting greater market valuations. Perhaps, the biggest of these is fostering a sense of cohesion among various team members and preventing situations where members of the senior management are not aligned to a common goal. Building one brand identity ushers in a feeling of unity and the desire to further a common vision that applies to all the team members working within the group. And the bigger and more diverse the group, the more critical this becomes.

It is also important here to recognize that the brand-building activity was taken up by Mr Ratan Tata even though it was in direct opposition to what his predecessor, Mr J.R.D. Tata, had furthered. Mr J.R.D. Tata had, in essence, taken the opposite step by allowing business leaders to head their specific units and take decisions independently. During his tenure, it made sense for the various Group companies to operate with a sense of independence due to the environment, which discouraged and regulated the growth of groups by licences.

However, the business tide had changed after Mr Ratan Tata became the chairman. He thought that it would more effective to tie in the individual entities with the thread of an all-encompassing brand identity, and he proceeded to do what he believed was the best move for ensuring the success of the Group. Aside from being a smart business move, it is also an admirable example of the flexibility that a business leader must exhibit to rebuild the organization, even if it actually means to demolish the structure which has caused it to be successful in the first place! This has been formulated in an article by Larry Greiner where he states that as organizations evolve across five stages of growth, they will hit a ceiling at each stage, where they will stagnate.[21] The organizations will then have to have a revolution of sorts, where the existing structure, which had made the organization successful to date, will have to be demolished and a new structure will have to be built. This new structure will then help the organization grow to the next level. This can be clearly seen in the case of the Tatas where successive chairmen have worked on changing the structure of the Group to make it more adaptive to the changing environment, and thus, ensuring the long-term growth and success of the Group.

---

[21]Larry E. Greiner, 'Evolution and revolution as organizations grow', *Harvard Business Review*, 76:3 (1998): 55–64

3

GROW IN THE RIGHT SPIRIT: DOING THE RIGHT THINGS RIGHT LIKE THE TATAS

AN UPRIGHT MORAL STANDING AND COMPLIANCE IN FINANCIAL MATTERS ARE YOUR BUSINESS'S BEST FRIENDS.

What would have happened if our philosophy was like that of some other companies which do not stop at any means to attain ends... If we were like other groups we would be twice as big as they are today. What we have sacrificed is a 100 per cent growth, but we wouldn't want it any other way.

—Mr J.R.D. Tata[22]

---

[22]R.M. Lala, *The Creation of Wealth: The Tatas from the 19th to the 21st Century*, Penguin Random House India Private Limited, 2004, Kindle edition

Say 'Tatas', and scores of people come up with very positive adjectives to describe the Group: honest, fair and transparent. As a business empire, the Tata Group has become renowned for adhering to its principles, even in the face of adversity. The senior leadership prides itself in being driven by values and maintaining a strict adherence to an ethical code of conduct.[23] It has been this approach to business that has consistently upheld the Group's reputation as an entity that can be trusted.

PRIORITIZING TAX COMPLIANCE

Keeping their records clean and complying with the laws are prerequisites for conducting ethical business. On this dimension, the Tata Group has shown exemplary dedication.

R.M. Lala, in his book titled *The Creation of Wealth: The Tatas from the 19th to the 21st Century*, shares an incident that exemplifies the distance that the Tatas are willing to go to maintain transparency.[24]

Mr Dinesh Vyas, who is acknowledged as one of India's best-known tax consultants, used to consult with the Tata Group at the time. He recalls a story where a senior Tata executive recommended a tax avoidance method that would help the company save on taxes. Before the case was put up, the chairman of the company took this matter to Mr J.R.D.,

---

[23]https://www.tata.com/about-us/tata-values-purpose, accessed 10 March 2019

[24]R.M. Lala, *The Creation of Wealth: The Tatas from the 19th to the 21st Century*, Penguin Random House India Private Limited, Kindle edition, Location 171 of 3790

who was the Group chairman then. Mr Vyas had stated his opinion to Mr J.R.D. Tata that the tax-saving recommendation was not illegal. But the response he received from the Group chairman caught him unaware. Mr Vyas admits never to have witnessed such a reaction in his long years of experience as a tax consultant.

'Not illegal, yes,' said Mr J.R.D. Tata. *'But is it right?'*

Mr Vyas, while sharing his experiences in the book, stated that Mr J.R.D. Tata never debated terms like 'tax avoidance' (which is legal and permissible) or 'tax evasion' (which is illegal). Instead, he had a single-minded motto that he always propagated. It was 'tax compliance'.

Clearly, Mr J.R.D. Tata preferred to err on the side of caution, and did not even consider options that did not meet his strict standards of tax compliance. He did not wish to take any chances with unclear matters that presented any scope for disagreement on legal and financial fronts. With him, tax compliance was the straightforward route to opt for, no matter what the costs.

A similar preference to adhere to compliances and being financially prudent and conservative can be seen throughout the history of the Tata Group. The Tatas have traditionally preferred to be upfront and conduct their business with integrity, especially in monetary matters. For instance, in 1924, Sir Dorabji Tata risked his entire fortune of ₹1 crore (approximately ₹90 crore as per 2019 values) only to get a loan from the State Bank of India (SBI). He wanted this loan for Tata Steel that did not have enough money to pay salaries to its workers. The primary motive behind this action was to retain the goodwill of the Tata Group and avoid a default. For Sir Dorabji Tata, it was worth risking everything he owned only to ensure that the business never faltered on its commitments.

The Tata's commitment to doing the right things the right way has been fruitful in the long run. Not only has it given the Group an impressive reputation as being a veritable and upright business house, but it has also circumvented potentially sticky situations. An incident that happened to a Tata employee throws light on the unmovable ethical stand that the Tata Group has built and propounded.[25] A Tata employee was returning to India from a foreign trip in 1969. He was carrying a bag full of cheap pens and toys as souvenirs for his colleagues bought from a Chinese emporium. The goods were not too expensive. However, he could not furnish the bill to the customs authorities to prove that the goods had cost below ₹500, the permissible limit at the time. It was quite a situation, and intensive questioning ensued.

By now, a senior customs officer had been called. He asked the passenger where he worked. 'Tata Steel,' he replied. Upon hearing this response, the senior customs officer started to help the passenger pack the goods back into his travel bag! He must be speaking the truth, explained the officer to the customs agent, as he was convinced that the Tata people always told the truth!

While this incident may be anecdotal, it does throw light on the solid public perception of the Group—an image that

---

[25] Arun Maira, 'The Tatas and a matter of trust', LiveMint, 3 November 2016, accessed 7 April 2019, https://www.livemint.com/Opinion/GOx9Ym0MSLSGwbHb6WSvsO/The-Tatas-and-a-matter-of-trust.html,

has been built over time because of its leaders' unflinching devotion to keeping values and integrity uncompromised and expecting the same from their people in all their dealings.

Amidst this, one question becomes apparent: why and how does the Tata Group manage to uphold such strict ethical standards? Part of the answer, perhaps, lies in the core purpose that the Tatas have identified for themselves. As a divisional head had been quoted in an interview with *The Economist* in 2012, 'Return on capital is not at the centre of our business. Our purpose is nation-building, employment and acquiring technical skills.'[26]

Mr J.R.D. Tata also agrees with this core purpose, explaining that the Tata Group believed in the spirit of trusteeship—'to act as trustees and to consider major problems of the country in connection with the firm as trustees and not as businessmen merely trying to make money for the firm.'[27] He further said:

> The Tatas are in fact a trust and an institution more than just a business house. Right from the early days I knew Mahatma Gandhi and I was quite impressed and believed in the spirit of trusteeship... Incidentally, we want to make money because that is the only way to make funds available to charitable trusts.[28]

---

[26]'From pupil to master', *The Economist*, 1 December 2012, accessed 25 May 2019, https://www.economist.com/business/2012/12/01/from-pupil-to-master

[27]Sundar Sarukkai, 'JRD Tata and the Idea of Trusteeship', 2012, accessed 24 April 2019, http://eprints.manipal.edu/78163/1/Zoroastrianism_-_JRD_Tata_%26_the_idea_of_trusteeship-_SS-textbook.pdf

[28]Ibid.

TAKEAWAY

In the modern world, it has almost become fashionable to associate business with shrewdness. It is frequently recommended that business leaders become street-smart, consider short-term gains, save money where they can, go around problems and financial challenges rather than try to tackle things head-on. The Tata Group is arguably one of the most well-established and successful business groups in the country, and yet, its adherence to all things straightforward has become the subject of admiration. This is also the reason why reputed international companies have partnered with the Tata Group.

The people at the helm in the Tata Group have adhered to ethical practices for decades, and it is this strong belief in values and non-compromising attitude to any 'bending' of the rules that have been instrumental in achieving their business success. The clean image of the Tatas precedes them; it extends far beyond the tenures of the individual chairpersons or the independent companies.

Another lesson worth noting here is that the Tata Group has been consistent over decades, when it comes to growing in the right spirit. Many companies that have otherwise been transparent tend to lose their standing when they operate in uncertain and regulated environments or over time. Some of them resort to bribing government officials to get their work done. But decisions like these, more often than not, prove counterproductive over time. Incurring a few losses in the present is preferable to suffering a severe loss of reputation and the threat of being blacklisted some years down the line.

The Tata Group has adopted this route, and even though it has been blamed for reduced performance of some of its companies, it has remained steadfast on its chosen path. An article in the May-June issue of the *Harvard Business Review*, states that leaders in the best ethical organizations have designed their environments for encouraging ethical behaviour by keeping ethical principles foremost, using formal and informal incentives and opportunities for rewarding ethics and making ethics an integral part of day-to-day behaviour.[29] And the Tatas seem to be miles ahead of the others in actually having practised this over the years!

In this regard, the Tata Group is an example worth emulating. In fact, there have been some reported cases where regulatory officers have been advised against asking for a bribe when it was a Tata company on the other side of the table. A Tata company would not pay a bribe, so broaching the subject would be futile and potentially dangerous, as the Group is not afraid to fight for what is right.

---

[29]Nicholas Epley and Amit Kumar, 'How to design an Ethical Organisation', May–June 2019, *Harvard Business Review*, page 150

4
TREAT PATIENCE AS A VIRTUE

BEING PATIENT IN BUSINESS DECISIONS AND WAITING FOR RESULTS TO SHOW SHOULD BE SECOND NATURE TO A MANAGER.

Business is often associated with an aggressive attitude to achieve results at any costs. In the midst of this, a simple, humble virtue like patience doesn't get the attention it deserves. What good is patience in an environment where competitors use every means possible to move ahead and combat your best moves? As the Tata Group has demonstrated over time, patience is not only a good trait to have for a manager, but it is also an essential virtue determining the way the Group operates.

In their illustrious history, the Tatas have frequently faced adversity and rejection. Often, this has been due to restrictions imposed by the government. Hurdles put up by legal authorities and the slow (or sometimes complete absence of) arrivals of government permissions have thwarted the Group's business plans. But the Tatas have refused to let such rejections discourage their efforts towards business—and nation-building. Instead, they have preferred to wait and be patient.

LOST OPPORTUNITIES, LONG DELAYS

One of the earliest instances dates back to 1967 when Mr Darbari Seth of Tata Chemicals made a presentation to Mrs Indira Gandhi, who was then the prime minister of India. The presentation was for a fertilizer project, which, in the long term, would be converted into an agro-industrial complex. Mrs Gandhi had reportedly been excited by the conceptual scope of the project and its potential role in developing the Indian economy. However, the permissions did not materialize. It is believed that some of Mrs Gandhi's advisors objected to this project, primarily because it might have been perceived as an unwarranted gesture of support to the Tatas.

The Tata Group has also faced multiple rejections in the automobile sector—something that seems quite impossible to fathom in today's reality when Tata Motors is one of the country's largest manufacturers of automobiles. In 1960, the Group was in talks with Mercedes-Benz, their truck partner, to manufacture the 180D model, the popular passenger vehicle, in India. But the permissions never came in; the reasons remain unknown till date. It is possible that this rejection caused a huge opportunity loss for greater economic development in the country.[30]

---

[30]Shashank Shah, *The Tata Group: From Torchbearers to Trailblazers*, Penguin Random House India, 2018, Kindle edition, Location 6411 of 8244

There were also multiple delays in the airline business—a sector that the Group had been eager to enter since early days. They had been the first company to launch Tata Airlines (which Mr J.R.D. Tata personally used to fly, carrying air mail from Karachi to Mumbai). This was later nationalized and rechristened to Air India in 1953. To further their interests in this sector, the Group made several applications to the government for the requisite licences. But these frequently got stuck—sometimes, at multiple stages. It was only in 2013 that the Tata's joint venture with Air Asia was approved. That year, Vistara, the Tata's joint venture with Singapore Airlines (SIA), was also approved.

THE INDICA STORY

In 1998, Mr Ratan Tata launched the Group's passenger car business with the maiden vehicle—a hatchback called Indica. While the launch was done, in all likelihood, with great expectations, the results were disappointing. The car failed to perform as expected, with several customers complaining about the product quality and engine performance. The Group resolved to address all the customer complaints, even if that meant incurring huge costs. That year, Tata Motors reported a net loss of ₹5 billion for the year 1999–2000.[31] It was not only the largest recorded loss in the history of the Tata Group,

---

[31] Rediff.com, 'Big mistakes that crashed Tata Motors ambitious car dream', 1 October 2014, accessed 25 May 2019, https://www.rediff.com/money/report/pix-auto-big-mistakes-that-crashed-tata-motors-ambitious-car-dream/20141001.htm

but it was also among the largest losses ever declared by any private sector company in India.

In 1999, within a year of Indica's launch, the Group was looking to exit the sector. Ford Motor had expressed an interest in forging a deal. But something unsettling happened when the Tatas went to Detroit, USA, to work out the details of the deal. Reportedly, the Group underwent humiliation at the Ford office, with the officials telling them that they would be 'doing the Tatas a favour' by buying out the car division. Mr Pravin Kadle, a member of the Tata team at the time, confesses that the Tatas were also reprimanded for starting a passenger car division when they 'did not know anything'.[32] Mr Ratan Tata and his team returned to New York the very same day. It was allegedly a quiet flight. The sale was not been made.

Under the guidance of Mr Ratan Tata, the Group concentrated its energies in working on the next model of the 'failed' car—the Indica V2. As it turned out, the result was a much-improved car that subsequently changed the fortunes of the Group, becoming the second-largest selling hatchback in India by 2004.[33] The passenger car business had finally taken off, thus establishing Tata Motors' credentials as an automobile manufacturer.

---

[32]PTI, 'When "humiliated" Ratan Tata did "favour" to Ford with JLR buyout!' *The Economic Times*, 15 March 2015, accessed 12 April 2019, https://economictimes.indiatimes.com/industry/when-humiliated-ratan-tata-did-favour-to-ford-with-jlr-buyout/articleshow/46572012.cms

[33]Rediff.com, 'Big mistakes that crashed Tata Motors ambitious car dream', 1 October 2014, accessed 25 May 2019, https://www.rediff.com/money/report/pix-auto-big-mistakes-that-crashed-tata-motors-ambitious-car-dream/20141001.htm

It so happened that during the financial crisis of 2008, Ford Motor faced severe challenges. In fact, it went nearly bankrupt. During this time, Ford's Jaguar Land Rover division went up for sale. The Tatas bought it for $2.3 billion in 2008.[34] Mr Kadle recalls the exact words that Mr William Clay Ford Jr 'Bill' Ford, the chairman of Ford Motor addressed to Mr Ratan Tata during that meeting: 'You are doing us a favour by buying JLR.'[35]

From 1999 to 2008, life had turned full circle for the Tatas. The slow but steady success of their passenger vehicle division has been the result of patience and perseverance. Imagine how different the face of Tata Motors would have been today had the company given up hope and decided to wrap up!

TAKEAWAY

The Tatas have faced many disappointments in the course of business. But they have worked hard not to let these setbacks pull them down. As a business empire, the Tata Group has remained steady in its path towards progress and nation-building, even when toiling along that path has seemed an uphill task.

In exercising patience in business, the Tatas have also displayed a strong intention to comply with the law of the

---

[34]PTI, 'When "humiliated" Ratan Tata did "favour" to Ford with JLR buyout!' *The Economic Times*, 15 March 2015, accessed 12 April 2019, https://economictimes.indiatimes.com/industry/when-humiliated-ratan-tata-did-favour-to-ford-with-jlr-buyout/articleshow/46572012.cms
[35]Ibid.

land. The business world can abound with grey opportunities and shortcuts that achieve quick, if not exactly 'proper', results. But the Tatas have steered clear of such shortcuts and opted for the longer and more difficult route. This is a deliberate business strategy that might have slowed down growth but has ensured that when success arrives, it is more stable and sustainable.

In business—as in life—leaders are often faced with difficult choices and adverse conditions. While dubious shortcuts might lead to rapid growth, the slower path of integrity produces sustainable and longer-lasting results. It is vital to note here that consistent performers are usually those who opt for the latter and, in turn, end up with an enviable reputation and market credibility.

5
CHOOSE YOUR INDUSTRIES STRATEGICALLY

ENTER INDUSTRIES THAT YOU BELIEVE YOU CAN SUCCEED IN, BUT DO NOT ADOPT ANY MEASURES THAT CAN BECOME YOUR UNDOING.

'From salt to software'—that is how the Tata Group is described by market watchers and analysts around the globe. And that's no wonder, for the Group is present in multiple industries, many of them as different as chalk and cheese. The Group is among the first choices for many foreign companies looking to enter the Indian market. In fact, the Tata Group's list of partners reads like a veritable global blue chip company's list! Having valuable partners alongside has enabled the Group to enter several industries quickly, for example, IBM, Daimler-Benz, Sky TV, Hitachi, Cummins, etc. However, the Group has refrained from taking hasty decisions just because it could. It has instead kept its entry strategies into various industries well-considered and slow.

CHOOSING TO MAINTAIN A DISTANCE

Let us take up some examples of industries that the Tata Group has consciously remained away from and why. For starters, the Group did not enter the infrastructure industry even when an opportunity presented itself. Mr Ratan Tata explained the rationale behind this: a pure case of profitability. Mr Ratan Tata observed that in the infrastructure sector, the tendency was to bid for contracts at ridiculously low terms. This was because most government contracts were awarded to the lowest bidder. It often happened that the winner of the contract tried to renegotiate at a later stage. This clearly ambiguous scenario wasn't something in which the Tatas wished to dabble.

The Tata Group has also cautiously stayed away from businesses such as cigarettes and alcohol, or businesses that are prone to corruption. Mr Farokh N. Subedar, the Chief Operating Officer (COO) of Tata Sons, once stated that this was a deliberate decision. The Tatas recognized that they would not succeed in such businesses, as their approach would always become a handicap.[36]

> Today, the Tatas represent assurance, reliability, a sense of nationalism, value for money... Irrespective of the product you are making, those are the attributes

---

[36]Shashank Shah, *The Tata Group: From Torchbearers to Trailblazers*, Penguin Random House India, 2018, Kindle edition, Chapter 5

you would like to be known for, whether it is through a wristwatch, a piece of software or a car.[37]

—Mr R. Gopalakrishnan,
Executive Director, Tata Sons

CHARTING THE AVIATION SECTOR

The Tatas had long displayed a desire to enter the aviation sector in India. The Group had made multiple attempts to start a domestic airline, especially after the nationalization of Tata Airlines. This can be partly attributed to Mr J.R.D. Tata's passion for the aviation industry—a proclivity that was also shared to an extent by Mr Ratan Tata.

To this end, the Group entered into multiple rounds of discussions with the government. On several occasions, the permissions seemed to be in sight, almost like the light at the end of a dark tunnel. In 2001, the government announced that it was considering disinvesting 40 per cent stake in Air India,[38] and the Tatas had been asked to bid. Further to this, the Tatas collaborated with SIA to study the feasibility of a joint bid. When the bid finally took place in 2001, the Tatas were the sole bidders and appeared to have won. But, curiously, the bid was stopped in its tracks. The public press thought that it was due to rising public opposition fuelled by rival airline

---

[37]Rina Chandran, 'Revitalising Brand Tata', *Business Line*, 9 January 2003, accessed 7 April 2019, https://www.thehindubusinessline.com/catalyst/2003/01/09/stories/2003010900200100.htm

[38]Gargi Parsai, 'Airline disinvestment runs into rough weather', *The Hindu*, 8 July 2001, accessed 25 May 2019, http://www.thehindu.com/2001/07/08/stories/0508134a.htm

lobbyists and labour unions.[39] Mr Ratan Tata was forced to write to the government and withdraw his application since it had taken a very long time and SIA had withdrawn citing the long delay.[40]

The Tata Group's failed attempt at charting the aviation sector was regrettable. Although the Tatas had been pioneers in Indian aviation, the Group still faced massive hurdles in securing approvals to start a domestic airline.[41] Mr Ratan Tata confessed having approached three prime ministers of India, over the years, but Mr Tata's efforts were consistently blocked due to the efforts of one individual.

A decade later, Mr Ratan Tata recounted a meeting with a fellow industrialist to discuss the failed airline bid. The industrialist had, allegedly, rebuked Mr Ratan Tata for not paying a bribe of ₹15 crore that had been demanded by some of the authorities at the time for approving the permission for the airline. Mr Ratan Tata, although displeased and disappointed by how the whole thing had turned out, did not regret his decision. He admitted that it would have been impossible for him to go to bed at night knowing that he had set up an airline after paying a bribe of ₹15 crore. What he *did* regret, however, was that the vested interests of a few

---

[39]Shashank Shah, *The Tata Group: From Torchbearers to Trailblazers*, Penguin Random House India, 2018

[40]Bureau Report, 'No fresh bidding on Air India now–Tatas say goodbye after failure to find partner', *Business Line*, 8 December, 2001, accessed 25 May 2019, https://www.thehindubusinessline.com/2001/12/08/stories/1408043u.htm

[41]Shashank Shah, *The Tata Group: From Torchbearers to Trailblazers*, Penguin Random House India Private Limited, 2018, Kindle edition

groups had denied the country the benefits of a world-class competitive airline.[42]

MAINTAINING INTEGRITY IN THE FACE OF BUREAUCRATIC CONTROL

During the post-Independence period in India, several regulations were rolled out to control the growth of the private sector. The government nationalized all industries that it deemed to be in the public interest. This list included banks, insurance companies and airlines. The government also established strict controls on the setting up of new companies, while controlling the production and expansion capabilities of the existing ones. In the early '70s, income tax rates were as high at 98.75 per cent![43] In addition, there was a 'wealth tax' to be paid, which pushed the taxation rate to well over 100 per cent.

Understandably, these incredulous rates of taxation did not go down well with most entrepreneurs and businessmen. In response, many of them brainstormed 'ingenious' ways to 'manage' the system. If the government was using delays in granting permissions as a bureaucratic tool, bribing their way

---

[42] PTI, 'Tatas won't get into airline business: Ratan Tata', *The Economic Times*, 9 December 2012, accessed 25 May 2019, https://economictimes.indiatimes.com/industry/transportation/airlines-/-aviation/tatas-wont-get-into-airline-business-ratan-tata/articleshow/17544501.cms?from=mdr

[43] Prabhakar Sinha and Shankar Raghuraman, 'Level of tax rates rose in Indira regime', *The Times of India*, 4 March 2008, accessed 25 May 2019, https://timesofindia.indiatimes.com/business/india-business/Level-of-tax-rates-rose-in-Indira-regime/articleshow/2835227.cms

in was only a fitting response to overcome delays, as some businesses found out.

Amidst all this, the Tata Group remained solid. The Group's airline experience is a classic example of a potentially good proposal being held up in the government bureaucracy. However, the Tatas preferred to wait it out and did not consider using other means to 'speed up' their entry into the new industry by resorting to bribes or other under-the-table favours. This approach has been consistent throughout their business history, across the Group companies. For instance, the Group has often had to incur delays on government orders for regulating the output of Tata Steel and Tata Motors. But the endeavour has always been to maintain integrity and professionalism.

TAKEAWAY

To fuel business growth, the Tatas have diversified and entered into various industries. Many of these entries have been fraught with challenges, not the least of which has been obtaining the required permissions from the government. But the Tatas consciously chose an entry strategy of integrity and patience. While their decisions were strategic and fuelled by passion, as in the case of their proposed airline venture, the Group steadfastly refused to succumb to the temptation of bribery.

In business, managers often have to make trade-offs. Sometimes, an entry strategy into a new industry might be slow only because it is straightforward and 'correct'. Adopting this approach might mean that competitors run past you since they have found ways to circumvent the hurdles that bog you down. However, the slow and considered pathway usually turns out to be longer lasting. The Tatas accepted the temporary handicap of slower growth with grace, agreeing to wait until the tide turned in their favour. And if it didn't, they accepted the situation as an opportunity that wasn't meant to be.

The Tata Group, in spite of the best intentions, has often been subject to political pressures and attacks from various quarters; for example, the Airline case above, or the Tata Chemicals permissions being denied. This has partly been due to their sheer size and dominance in the business world. The Tata senior leaders have endeavoured to respond to the stakeholders to keep them reassured and invested, by planning not only for the present but also for the years to come. It is safe to infer that this was a more mature viewpoint than attempting to manipulate permissions or sanctions. It also reflects the intelligence of keeping one's eyes set on the future instead of being swayed by short-term setbacks.

It is possible that if the Tata Group had chosen the path of sheer profit, the revenues and profits of some of the Group companies could have been higher. But this would have meant lower allocation for the philanthropy and welfare projects that it engages in. In other words, the Tatas would be putting at stake the thousands of lives they had touched over the years and incurring a serious loss to the socio-economic development of India. One doubts if this trade-off would have been acceptable to the Tatas.

6

BUILD TRUST IN YOUR BUSINESS TO GROW YOUR BUSINESS

A SENSE OF TRUST IN YOUR BUSINESS IS THE MOST VALUABLE GIFT OF ALL; ALWAYS MAKE ATTEMPTS TO GROW IT WITH ALL THE STAKEHOLDERS.

If there is one blessing that the Tata Group genuinely enjoys, it is the sense of trust that it inspires among the masses. The Group is well respected not only among its employees but also among market watchers, analysts and business associates. However, while this level of faith is indeed an asset, it is one that the Group has nurtured over time. It is essentially the Tata's actions—one careful and considerate act at a time—that has resulted in such deeply engrained trust.

In Chapter 3, we discussed one crucial instance that exemplifies the Tata Group's commitment to being honest and transparent: Mr J.R.D. Tata and his thoughts on tax avoidance. In his book, Mr Lala discussed how a senior tax executive's recommendation on 'avoiding' taxes was dismissed by Mr J.R.D. Tata. This was all because neither the executive nor Mr Dinesh Vyas, the Tata's tax consultant at the time, had a convincing answer to his simple question: the suggested tax-saving approach may not be illegal, but was it *right*? The firm hold on integrity that the Group's leaders have always possessed has been instrumental in building immense trust in the Group's actions. Let us take a few more important examples to understand the Tata Group's attitude towards trust building.

THE KRAUSSMAFFEI INCIDENT

In 1946, the Board of KraussMaffei, a German engineering conglomerate, met Mr J.R.D. Tata and Mr Sumant Moolgaokar, the then CEO of TELCO, which was at that time a small company.[44] The meeting took place in Munich, soon after the end of the Second World War. KraussMaffei was in doldrums; many of their German engineers were starving because there was no work available in post-war Germany.

During the meeting, the Board requested the Tatas to hire their best engineers and technicians, and relocate them along with their families to India. However, this was impossible. As India was under British rule at the time, there was no possibility of an Indian company being allowed to make any business agreements with German companies. The Board,

---

[44] Arun Maira, 'The Tatas and a matter of trust', LiveMint, 3 November 2016, accessed 7 April 2019, https://www.livemint.com/Opinion/GOx9Ym0MSLSGwbHb6WSvsO/The-Tatas-and-a-matter-of-trust.html,

although understandably disappointed, requested the Tatas to take their best technicians and their families to India, as they were starving without any work in Germany. All that the Germans asked was that the Tatas take care of the workers who would teach them all they knew. The Tatas agreed and soon they were trained in metal working by some of the best engineers in Germany.

Shortly after, in 1947, India secured independence. A letter arrived at the KraussMaffei headquarters. It was from the Tatas and asked only one question: Now that they (the Tatas) could pay, how much should the Tatas pay for the technology that they had got from the Germans?

The KraussMaffei Board maintains that this action defines the true essence of trust. Trust gets built when one honours one's debts—even when it is not legally binding to do so, or even when it is not demanded.

TATA STARBUCKS: A WINNING EXERCISE IN TRUST

In 2014, Mr Howard Schultz, Chairman, President and CEO of Starbucks Coffee Company, gave an interview to *McKinsey Quarterly* about the performance of the famous coffee chain in India. In his interview, he stated what he felt was the top reason for his company's success in the country: partnering with the Tatas.[45]

---

[45] Howard Schultz and Miles White, 'Reimaging India: Creating partnerships for the future', *McKinsey Quarterly*, January 2014, accessed 27 April 2019, https://www.mckinsey.com/featured-insights/asia-pacific/reimagining-india-creating-partnerships-for-the-future

It is interesting to note that Starbucks always had the option to enter the Indian market on its own, a little later on. The government regulation had changed within a few months of Starbucks's announcement of a joint venture with the Tatas. But Mr Schultz preferred not to go about it alone—a move towards which he has since expressed being happy about. In his interview, he lavishly praised the support that Starbucks had received from the Tatas. He even admitted that it would have been unimaginable even to consider entering India without this kind of support!

Notably, though, such a strong relationship between the two businesses did not develop overnight. The Tatas invested monumental effort into making this joint venture a success:

- The Tata Group worked on the locations, menu choices, recruitment, store design, and logistical and infrastructural hurdles. It ensured that fresh food was offered on the menu.
- The joint venture was able to source and roast coffee beans locally in India in Tata-owned roasting facilities.
- Starbucks developed an India-only espresso roast that was designed especially for Indian audiences. For the first time ever in the history of Starbucks, this blend was roasted not by the Starbucks team, but by the Tatas. Starbucks had trusted the Tatas with their roasting secrets; they had guarded these secrets with their life for over forty years.

Mr Howard Schultz excellently summarized the foundation of the association in his interview:

In the process, we learned that not everything needs to be invented in Seattle, and that with the right partner, we can collaborate and coauthor, as long as there is a foundation of trust.[46]

TAKEAWAY

The most significant learning from this lesson is the steady manner in which the Tata Group has developed trust in its dealings—a concerted effort that every business leader needs to spearhead to achieve success. As a business empire, the Group has consistently behaved in a trustworthy manner, going the extra mile to showcase integrity, even when it wasn't strictly mandatory to do so.

It is certainly possible that in the $100-billion empire, there may be employees or executives not following this principle of trust. However, what is important to remember is that the message from the top has always been the same: all the employees *must* behave with integrity and fairness. This behaviour of doing what is right and fair has become deeply ingrained in the fabric of the Tata Group, and it is this that has helped them earn incomparable goodwill from their partners. The Starbucks instance is a powerful demonstration of the response that such goodwill can achieve. The company did the inconceivable by sharing its trade secrets and processes that

---

[46]Howard Schultz and Miles White, 'Reimaging India: Creating partnerships for the future', *McKinsey Quarterly*, January 2014, accessed 27 April 2019, https://www.mckinsey.com/featured-insights/asia-pacific/reimagining-india-creating-partnerships-for-the-future

are at the heart of its intellectual property; these are also its key assets that are not shared with anyone but an entity that enjoys unconditional trust.

As managers, it is imperative to begin trust-building exercises early on. Cementing one's reputation as a firm with integrity and strong core values takes time and one has to work on it continuously over the long term. It is a long-term proposition that is replete with the temptation to grab shortcuts and skimp on the immediate sacrifices. In such situations, one can take a leaf from the Tata book and focus on building an empire brick by brick, on a solid foundation. The rewards will be abundant. One of the biggest rewards will be high-quality partners who prefer to work with firms that epitomize trust over just short-term profits.

7

FACE ADVERSITY HEAD-ON: THE TATA-DOCOMO SAGA

THE STICKIEST OF SITUATIONS CAN OFTEN BE RESOLVED BY STRAIGHTFORWARD TACTICS, AS LONG AS YOU MAINTAIN YOUR CORE VALUES.

In the eventful history of the Tata Group, there have been numerous instances of turmoil. These adverse situations—some of which could have blown over a lesser company—have taught the Group to emerge stronger and more resilient. Let us study in detail one such incident that has abundant lessons in tackling the vicissitudes of business: the Tata-DoCoMo saga.

THE TATA-DOCOMO ARBITRATION AWARD

In 2009, DoCoMo, the partner of Tata Teleservices Ltd (TTSL), sold a 26.5 per cent stake to NTT DoCoMo for $2.7

billion.[47,48] NTT DoCoMo is a leading mobile phone operator in Japan. At the time, the shareholders' agreement entered into by the two parties clearly dictated some strict terms. If TTSL did not achieve the set performance targets in the subsequent five years, the Tatas would have to find a buyer for DoCoMo's shares. The shares would then be sold at market prices. If, however, they failed to find a buyer, the Tatas would buy the shares at a 50 per cent discounted price.

By 2014, that is five years later, TTSL had failed to achieve its performance targets. DoCoMo announced its plans to exit India and also wanted to sell its shares.

To this end, the Tatas asked for the requisite permission from the Reserve Bank of India (RBI). However, the RBI refused permission on the grounds that such a transfer of funds violated the provisions of the Foreign Exchange Management Act (FEMA), 1999. It was, according to the RBI, against public policy.[49]

DoCoMo turned to the arbitration route. The London

---

[47] Vikrant Rana and Sudipto Mitra, 'The Tata DOCOMO Case: A coping Mechanism or a cop out plan?' Mondaq, 18 May 2017, accessed 27 April 2019, http://www.mondaq.com/india/x/595536/Contract+Law/The+Tata+DOCOMO+Case+A+Coping+Mechanism+Or+A+Cop+Out+Plan

[48] Bureau Report, 'Tata Sons pays NTT DoCoMo $1.2b, settles 3-year old dispute', *The Hindu BusinessLine*, 31 October 2017, accessed 27 April 2019, https://www.thehindubusinessline.com/info-tech/tata-sons-pays-ntt-docomo-12-b-settles-3yearold-dispute/article9935449.ece

[49] Shally Seth Mohile, 'Tata-Docomo dispute settled as Tata Sons pays $1.27 bn arbitration award', LiveMint, 1 November 2017, accessed 27 April 2019, https://www.livemint.com/Industry/OEfLrYc0PPUT5i3oOBN1ZL/NTT-Docomo-gets-12-billion-payment-from-Tata-Sons-dispute.html

Court of International Arbitration (LCIA) awarded DoCoMo $1.17 billion as damage charges for breach of contract. DoCoMo then moved the Delhi High Court to implement the award. However, the RBI rules prevented the Tatas from paying it.[50,51]

It was a sticky situation that could easily snowball into a corporate scandal. The Tatas were, quite naturally, unhappy with the mess. They were also displeased with the multiple cases being filed against them in the US and UK courts.[52,53] It is alleged that Mr Ratan Tata was even considering suing the Japanese firm for defamation. The DoCoMo issue has also been reported to be a point of contention during Mr Cyrus Mistry's tenure as the chairman.

Eventually, the Tatas, unwilling to lose their firm hold on integrity in the face of turmoil, took a concrete step. In March

---

[50]Shally Seth Mohile, 'Tata-Docomo dispute settled as Tata Sons pays $1.27 bn arbitration award', LiveMint, 1 November 2017

[51]ET Bureau, 'Cyrus Mistry and Tatas spar over DoCoMo case, Mistry says Ratan Tata was always kept in loop', *The Economic Times*, 2 November 2016, accessed 27 April 2019, https://economictimes.indiatimes.com/news/company/corporate-trends/cyrus-mistry-and-tatas-spar-over-docomo-case-mistry-says-ratan-tata-was-always-kept-in-loop/articleshow/55185615.cms

[52]Dev Chatterjee, 'Tata Sons wants quick resolution of DoCoMo issue', *Business Standard*, 27 October 2016, accessed 27 April 2019, https://www.business-standard.com/article/companies/did-handling-of-docomo-issue-lead-to-cyrus-mistry-ouster-116102501583_1.html

[53]Sayan Ghosal and Abhineet Kumar, 'DoCoMo case: Tata Sons moves London court', *Business Standard*, 6 September 2016, accessed 27 April 2019, https://www.business-standard.com/article/companies/tata-sons-moves-london-court-to-set-aside-ex-parte-order-by-docomo-116090500820_1.html

2017, Mr Ratan Tata led settlement talks with DoCoMo. This had been approved by the Tata Sons Board on 21 February 2017.[54] The Group deposited the full sum of the arbitral award (₹8,450 crore) with the registrar of the High Court.[55] Ultimately, in November 2017, the complete payment was made to DoCoMo, and the matter was finally settled.[56]

Subsequently, Tata Sons wrote off the entire investment of ₹286.5169 billion in Tata Teleservices, the loss-making telecom arm.[57] This was conducted according to the required regulatory filing norms. In October 2018, Tata Sons transferred the consumer mobile business of Tata Teleservices to Bharti Airtel. It was a debt-free, cash-free transaction made on the condition that Bharti Airtel would assume a fraction (₹2,000 crore of ₹10,000 crore) of the unpaid spectrum fees payable

---

[54]Shally Seth Mohile, 'How Ratan Tata changed track on Docomo to lead settlement talks', LiveMint, 1 March 2017, accessed on 27 April 2019, https://www.livemint.com/Companies/6hk3AyarCr4OexFCRQk1IM/Docomo-deal-How-Ratan-Tata-changed-track-to-lead-settlement.html

[55]Sayan Ghosal and Abhineet Kumar, 'DoCoMo case: Tata Sons moves London court', *Business Standard*, 6 September 2016, accessed 27 April 2019, https://www.business-standard.com/article/companies/tata-sons-moves-london-court-to-set-aside-ex-parte-order-by-docomo-116090500820_1.html

[56]Shally Seth Mohile, 'Tata-Docomo dispute settled as Tata Sons pays $1.27 bn arbitration award', LiveMint, 1 November 2017, accessed 27 April 2019, https://www.livemint.com/Industry/OEfLrYc0PPUT5i3oOBN1ZL/NTT-Docomo-gets-12-billion-payment-from-Tata-Sons-dispute.html

[57]PTI, 'Tata Sons writes off entire Rs 286-bn investment in Tata Teleservices', *Business Standard*, 22 October 2018, accessed 25 May 2019, https://www.business-standard.com/article/companies/tata-sons-writes-off-entire-rs-286-bn-investment-in-tata-teleservices-118102201180_1.html

to the Department of Telecommunications.[58,59] It was said that that the Tatas had effectively given away the core mobile business to Bharti Airtel, as a move to cut losses, instead of making huge investments needed to compete against well-established competitors.[60] Tata Sons also hived off the enterprise segment to merge with Tata Communications, the Group's networking arm. This finally ended the Tata-DoCoMo saga—a tumultuous episode in the Group's history that taught them indispensable lessons in dealing with adversity.

TAKEAWAY

The DoCoMo situation has a major lesson that all managers should learn upfront: the prudence of settling matters before they blow up and assume gigantic proportions. It is possible that the Tata-DoCoMo saga could have become uglier and resulted in the defamation or disruption in affairs of both parties involved. But timely intervention managed to nip the ugliness in the bud.

---

[58] Shally Seth Mohile, 'Tata-Docomo dispute settled as Tata Sons pays $1.27 bn arbitration award', Livemint, 1 November 2017, accessed 27 April 2019, https://www.livemint.com/Industry/OEfLrYc0PPUT5i3oOBN1ZL/NTT-Docomo-gets-12-billion-payment-from-Tata-Sons-dispute.html

[59] Amrit Raj, 'Airtel to buy Tata's consumer mobile business in a debt-free, cash-free deal', LiveMint, 13 October 2017, accessed 27 April 2019, https://www.livemint.com/Industry/np5deDZO690meWCzkVENJK/Bharti-Airtel-Tata-to-merge-consumer-mobile-businesses.html

[60] Amrit Raj, 'Airtel to buy Tata's consumer mobile business in a debt-free, cash-free deal', LiveMint, 13 October 2017, accessed 27 April 2019, https://www.livemint.com/Industry/np5deDZO690meWCzkVENJK/Bharti-Airtel-Tata-to-merge-consumer-mobile-businesses.html

The Tata's approach to tackling adversity also proves the power of integrity. The leadership found it preferable to arrive at a straightforward albeit expensive settlement instead of letting the situation become a stalemate.

It is true that despite adopting honest measures to deal with adversity, the Tata Group has been unable to avoid scandals completely. In 2008, when there was widespread furore in India over the skewed issuance of telecoms licences, the Tatas couldn't completely escape the brunt. There is some degree of speculation about the potential for 'funny business' somewhere in the $100-billion firm, but this remains a speculation. Meanwhile, the Tatas remain unscathed despite allegations, which have not been proven, hurled against them.

Perhaps the most scathing challenge that the Group faces is one posed by some rivals: persistent grumbling about the 'truth' of the Tata's relationship with the government. Some competitors claim that the Tata's current respectability masks a past spent toadying up to politicians, particularly in the years leading up to (and soon after) India's independence in 1947.

In dealing with these tortuous situations, the Tatas have used a basic but potent weapon: a steadfast moral standing. Many of the leading Tata men have stood against corruption in both private and professional dealings. While their attitude towards India's political issues has not been apathetic, it has often been one of polite distance. Mr Ratan Tata has, in particular, long attacked what he calls 'vested interests'. He believes that this terminology is a code for crony capitalism—a scenario in which firms make profits by buying favours from officials and politicians. By choosing to stay away from such murky waters, the Tata Group has demonstrated an effective strategy to maintain integrity inspite of adversity.

8

GROWTH BY ACQUISITION: THE TATA'S TAKEOVER STRATEGY

TAKEOVERS CAN BE AN EFFECTIVE STRATEGY FOR BUSINESS GROWTH, AS LONG AS YOU KEEP THE LARGER PICTURE IN PERSPECTIVE.

Traditionally, the Tatas had used the 'Greenfield Strategy' for growth. So, the Group had consistently set up new ventures and units from scratch. However, under the leadership of Mr Ratan Tata, the Group increasingly started to resort to a new strategy for expansion: takeovers. The business empire focused its energies on acquiring existing companies that it deemed to be a good fit. Many of these takeovers were on the global stage (see Annexure 1). In this chapter, let us study the guidelines that the Tata Group followed to make the takeover strategy for growth a success.

The Tata's rules for takeovers:

- Practise 'light touch and hands off'
- Win over people
- Invest in the community
- Retain local talent and premium brands
- Treat takeovers as partnerships, not acquisitions
- Train Indian managers
- Progress from 'you' and 'me' to 'we'

(The 'light touch and hands off' described the Tata's playbook for acquisitions, where they looked at acquisitions as a partnership and not just an acquisition. They preferred to retain the existing management and the identity of the original brands, keeping their interference to a minimum, nor imposing their needs on the organization. Under this, the older managements in the acquired company would be retained and given independence to operate but would be held accountable.)[61]

TATA CHEMICALS AND BRUNNER MOND

In June 2004, Tata Chemicals had acquired Hind Lever Chemicals Ltd (HLCL), an Indian company that manufactured bulk chemicals and phosphatic fertilizers.

In 2005, Tata Chemicals acquired the UK-based Brunner Mond Group, which was then one of the world's largest manufacturers and suppliers of soda ash. With plants in the UK, Netherlands and Kenya, Brunner Mond had the

---

[61]Shashank Shah, *The Tata Group: From Torchbearers to Trailblazers*, Penguin Random House India, 2018, page 192

capacity to manufacture 16 lakh tonne of soda ash. Its Kenya-based subsidiary—the Magadi Soda Company—had access to 'trona' (trisodium hydrogendicarbonate dehydrate), a naturally occurring mineral containing sodium carbonate compounds.

Brunner Mond was doing quite well in terms of acquisitions. Earlier in 2005, the company had acquired a stake in Indo Maroc Phosphore S.A., a Morocco-based firm.

The takeover of Brunner Mond was a strategic decision for Tata Chemicals. The former's access to trona offered a huge competitive advantage and could substantially reduce the net costs incurred by Tata Chemicals. The Magadi Soda Company's deposits of trona were among the purest surface deposits in the world and also the second largest.

However, the takeover deal didn't progress without its fair share of challenges. Uncertainties abounded among employees of all the three units across the UK, Kenya and India. The British were worried that the units would be sold off due to their high costs. The Kenyans worried about imminent closure since their units posed a threat to the Indian plants of Tata Chemicals. Their fears were not unfounded; many of them stemmed from the ill behaviour they had been used to in the hands of other Indian traders. There was resistance to the deal even back in India. The units at Mithapur, Gujarat were worried that they would be closed down on the grounds of poor cost competitiveness.

The Tata Chemicals team quickly sprung into action to mitigate these concerns. The team formulated a detailed integration plan with activities to be performed immediately, for the first hundred days, and beyond. It had the following basic tenets:

- Cross-functional teams would be formed with managers in all three locations.
- Managers would be brought in from Kenya to India so that they could understand the Tata culture.
- The Brunner Mond management would still retain operational control, while the Tatas would focus primarily on financial controls.

Let us examine this process in some more detail.

1. Immediate steps[62]

In the run-up to the takeover, the Tata Group conducted several one-on-one meetings with the key management officers of Brunner Mond and Magadi Soda. During these meetings, the following guidelines were established:

- All the senior employees and executives of the company would be retained.
- No change would be made in the company name, identity or reporting structures.
- The Tatas would consider the issues related to the Brunner Mond's pension plan; these liabilities were then a major concern for the company.

---

[62]Prashant Kale, Harbir Singh and Anand Raman, 'Don't Integrate your Acquisitions, Partner with them', *Harvard Business Review*, December 2009, accessed 27 April 2019, https://hbr.org/2009/12/dont-integrate-your-acquisitions-partner-with-them

- All post-acquisition decisions would be evaluated only after considering the best practices, processes and ideas from all the three companies. The best one on all fronts would be rolled out.

2. Steps in the first hundred days

In February 2006, the three parties chalked out a hundred-day plan to streamline the operations after the acquisition. This plan was formulated by a combined team of executives from all the three companies. The plan had a total of thirty-five primary tasks, including:

- Harmonizing the strategic planning process
- Planning how to handle the top global customers
- Aligning with the best human resources (HR) practices and policies
- Setting up protocols for communication and public relations (PR)

For the acquisition to be smooth and productive in the long run, Tata Chemicals assessed communication to be of prime significance. To this end, it formulated detailed guidelines which all the executives were expected to follow:

- Use every opportunity to talk about the TCC and the TBEM.
- Communicate the Tata Group's core business values and commitments to society.
- Mingle with your new colleagues and not just the employees of Tata Chemicals.

- Speak of 'coming together' and 'parentage' while avoiding terms like 'acquisition' and 'ownership'.
- Avoid terms like 'you' and 'us', focusing instead on the use of 'we'.

3. Steps taken in the long term

Finally, Tata Chemicals undertook the following organizational steps after the first hundred days:

- Setting up of a Global Chemicals Advisory Council to guide the organizational strategy and policies: This council was chaired by the managing director of Tata Chemicals along with eight senior members from all the three companies.
- Setting up of a three-member Business Heads Council: This would be responsible for coordinating operations, sales and marketing strategies. The chair would be determined by rotation.
- Sharing of data between the three companies, especially in situations when global customers needed to be approached.
- Assistance in sourcing equipment: Tata Chemicals helped Brunner Mond and Magadi Soda in sourcing the requisite materials for production from Indian suppliers.
- Discovering new business opportunities: The Tata Chemicals Innovation Centre in India and Brunner Mond's dedicated team for new ventures started working together to discover worthwhile business opportunities in Europe.

THE ACQUISITION OF JAGUAR LAND ROVER (JLR)

The Tata's acquisition of JLR is perhaps one of the most talked about deals in the business world. It is also a case study that abounds in takeover lessons for business leaders and managers. Let us examine the events leading up to the takeover and its results for all the parties involved.

Jaguar Land Rover was an automobile brand owned by the Ford Motor Company. In 1989, Ford acquired the Jaguar brand from the UK-based British Leyland by making several offers to the US and UK shareholders. The total purchase price was $2.5 billion.[63] Subsequently in 2000, Ford also acquired Land Rover in 2000 (from BMW) for $2.7 billion.[64]

But unfortunately for Ford, the company soon ran into huge losses in its core car manufacturing business in the US. The condition necessitated that Ford raise funds by selling some of its other assets. During the time that Ford owned Jaguar—1990 to 2008—it had attempted to fix the quality-related problems in its manufacturing units. The idea was that Jaguar should be able to compete with brands such as Mercedes-Benz and BMW. Competitors were investing in advanced features such as superior diesel engines and all-wheel-drive transmissions.[65]

---

[63]Shashank Shah, *The Tata Group: From Torchbearers to Trailblazers*, Penguin Random House India, 2018, page 146

[64]AFP, 'Mahindra drops out of Jaguar, Land Rover bid, Tata interested, says report', LiveMint, 14 September 2007, accessed 25 May 2019, https://www.livemint.com/Home-Page/c5XYtLdaGDMtQRqNFiu6nJ/Mahindra-drops-out-of-Jaguar-Land-Rover-bid-Tata-intereste.html

[65]Joan Muller, 'Jaguar's incredible turnaround and how it got ready to pounce on Tesla', *Forbes*, 7 March 2018, accessed 27 April 2007, https://www.forbes.com/sites/joannmuller/2018/03/07/jaguars-incredible-

Growth by Acquisition: The Tata's Takeover Strategy

Ford, however, failed to invest enough funds into technologies like these and Jaguar continued to make losses.

Just before the financial crisis of 2008, Ford offered JLR to the Tatas for $2.3 billion.[66] This was only about half of what Ford's purchase price had been. The Tatas were one of the many bidders for JLR but were allegedly the most favoured. This could have been due to the labour unions feeling that private equity players would slash jobs and resort to widespread layoffs to cut costs and improve performance. Hence, the British government, the JLR employees and the UK trade unions were interested in selling to the Tatas because of the belief that JLR would be looked after well by the Tatas.

In the year 2008, the financial crisis rocked the world. It hit the auto sector especially hard, shaking the business plans and strategies of many top players. During this time, Mr Ratan Tata focused on three things to make the JLR acquisition a success:

1. Managing the liquidity
2. Cutting costs by restructuring
3. Investing in new products to support future growth

To achieve these goals, Mr Ratan Tata gave a free hand to the JLR management team. A company executive admits that the Tatas gave JLR two perspectives—a long-term and a mid-

---

turnaround-and-how-it-got-ready-to-pounce-on-tesla/#5e188bc213c2
[66]Heather Timmons and Nick Bunkley, 'Ford Reaches Deal to Sell Land Rover and Jaguar', *The New York Times*, 27 March 2008, accessed 25 May 2019, https://www.nytimes.com/2008/03/27/business/worldbusiness/27auto.html

term one—along with the requisite money to realize both of these.[67] The Tata Group did not ask for dividends, preferring instead to reinvest in the business. As a result, JLR could start investing in new products. It managed to invest about 14 per cent of its revenues into research and development (R&D) and capital expenditures; the industry norm at the time was only about 5 per cent.[68]

The world, it seemed, realigned to give JLR's efforts a fillip. A key factor that turned around the fortunes of JLR to a large extent was the rising demand from Chinese consumers. But more importantly, the consumer preference saw a major shift from luxury cars to luxury sports utility vehicles (SUVs). Land Rover's SUVs were able to adjust quickly to the preferences of the luxury market. The Jaguar car, however, faced a challenge due to its retro design. It struggled to sell its vehicles—the XJ sedan and XK coupe.[69]

Mr Ratan Tata took a personal interest, working to lift the sales of Jaguar. He travelled across the US with his top management team and met the dealers of JLR. The idea was to get honest feedback for the products, straight from the horse's

---

[67] Joan Muller, 'Jaguar's incredible turnaround and how it got ready to pounce on Tesla', *Forbes*, 7 March 2018, accessed 27 April 2007, https://www.forbes.com/sites/joannmuller/2018/03/07/jaguars-incredible-turnaround-and-how-it-got-ready-to-pounce-on-tesla/#5e188bc213c2
[68] Ibid.
[69] *The Economic Times*, 'How Ratan Tata brought life to Jaguar Land Rover', *The Economic Times*, 10 March 2018, accessed 13 May 2019, https://economictimes.indiatimes.com/industry/auto/auto-news/how-ratan-tata-brought-life-to-jaguar-land-rover/working-from-ground-up/slideshow/63245737.cms

Growth by Acquisition: The Tata's Takeover Strategy

mouth. On his travels, Mr Ratan Tata managed to accumulate valuable product feedback and guidelines on how to improve sales. Back in India, he proceeded to translate these on the drawing board. The team quickly absorbed the feedback and adapted it into new, improved products.

The efforts of Mr Ratan Tata and his team paid off and how. The new cars were an instant success. In 2017, JLR won over 160 global awards, including the F-PACE winning the 'World Car of the Year' award.[70]

Going forward, JLR has announced multiple investments in Britain, India, China, Slovakia and Brazil. JLR also was planning to launch an electric vehicle that is alleged to compete against Tesla, an American automotive company specializing in electric car manufacturing. JLR's all-electric car, I-PACE, won three awards in 2019, including the World Car of the Year, World Car Design of the Year and World Green Car awards, becoming the first vehicle to win three categories.[71] Within the company is a sentiment of hope, with both the managers and the other employees optimistic about the future sales of JLR.

What the Tatas managed to do to JLR, retaining its British identity and still turn its fortunes around, is inspirational. In making this stiff task possible, the business leaders had to undertake several initiatives on a personal level. For instance,

---

[70]Company website, accessed 13 May 2019, https://www.jaguar.in/news/award-winning-vehicle.html

[71]Company website, accessed 13 May 2019, https://media.jaguar.com/en-gb/news/2019/04/jaguar-i-pace-wins-unprecedented-treble-2019-world-car-awards

it is reported that Mr Ratan Tata spent considerable time on the shop floor to oversee product development. This astonished the employees, most of whom had never seen any senior management officer on the shop floor, let alone the business owner himself. He also went the extra mile to ensure that the feedback received from the dealers in the US was implemented promptly. So, for example, the XF and XJ sedans received engines with increased efficiency—a popular demand among the customers. Not only did Mr Ratan Tata take the feedback very seriously, but he also guaranteed that there was minimal delay in absorbing this feedback across the board in the company. A US dealer admitted that the changes that had been incorporated into the JLR products in the following twelve to twenty-four months would have otherwise normally taken three to five years.[72]

The Tatas focused specifically on three areas:

i. Cash Management
ii. Cost Control
iii. New Product Development

To achieve these goals, the Tatas sold some stakes in its Group companies and came out with a rights offer. This was intended to raise funds in Tata Motors for JLR. They also controlled the liquidity in the short term to control costs in the middle term.

---

[72] *The Economic Times*, 'How Ratan Tata brought life to Jaguar Land Rover', *The Economic Times*, 10 March 2018, accessed 13 May 2019, https://economictimes.indiatimes.com/industry/auto/auto-news/how-ratan-tata-brought-life-to-jaguar-land-rover/working-from-ground-up/slideshow/63245737.cms

Growth by Acquisition: The Tata's Takeover Strategy

Over time, the Group planned investments in new models and worked on refurbishing of the old ones.

By the end of 2018, however, things had taken a downward trend. The sales of JLR started to decline. The XE and XF brands were not selling well, in spite of the best efforts of Mr Ralf Speth, a former BMW executive who had been hired to head JLR. Tata Motors, in a statement filed with the stock exchanges in India, disclosed that their financial results for the year ending 31 December 2018 had a one-time exceptional non-cash charge for asset impairment. This was a huge amount of £3.1 billion ($4 billion). Sales were down by 1.4 per cent. JLR also reduced 6,000 jobs and put 1,000 workers in the UK on a three-day work week. (The latter was part of a $3.2 billion cost-cutting plan named 'Project Charge').[73]

Let us examine the triggers of the downswing. Market experts attribute it primarily to[74, 75, 76]:

---

[73]Rishi Iyengar, 'Jaguar Land Rover causes biggest loss in Indian Corporate History', *CNN Business*, 8 February, 2019, accessed 20 April 2019, https://edition.cnn.com/2019/02/08/investing/tata-motors-jaguar-land-rover/index.html

[74]Outcome of the Board meeting, filed with the Bombay Stock Exchange (BSE), accessed 20 April 2019, https://www.bseindia.com/xml-data/corpfiling/AttachLive/6a66769e-c86d-4a11-a44b-cd90e393c077.pdf

[75]Automotive News Europe, 'Jaguar Land Rover takes $4.4B hit, writes down value of cars, plants', Automotive News Europe, 7 February 2019, accessed 20 April 2019, https://europe.autonews.com/automakers/jaguar-land-rover-takes-44b-hit-writes-down-value-cars-plants

[76]PR Sanjai, Ruth David, Tommaso Ebhardt and David Welch, 'Tata explores options for struggling Jaguar Land Rover', Bloomberg, 1 March 2019, accessed 20 April 2019, https://www.bloomberg.com/news/articles/2019-03-01/tata-is-said-to-explore-options-for-struggling-jaguar-land-rover

- Changing market conditions in China
- Inventory corrections
- US-China trade tensions
- The uncertainty around Brexit
- The low demand for diesel vehicles in Europe
- JLR's possibly overambitious attempts at competing head-on with BMW which was four times bigger in every segment

The scenario hit Tata Motors adversely as it relied on JLR for about 80 per cent of its sales and almost all of its profits.[77] A rumour started circulating that Tata Motors was seeking to divest its stake in JLR.[78] While the company responded to this immediately, refuting the story, it did express interest in finding an investor, a strategic partner or a sovereign wealth fund. The Group started looking to issue fresh equity.[79]

Presently, while Jaguar continues to suffer, Land Rover's products are doing well. Some Chinese dealers reportedly

---

[77] *The Economist*, 'Jaguar Land Rover is in a hole mostly of its own making', *The Economist*, 16 February 2019, accessed 20 April 2019, https://www.economist.com/business/2019/02/16/jaguar-land-rover-is-in-a-hole-mostly-of-its-own-making

[78] Tanvi Mehta, 'Tata denies it plans Jaguar Land Rover Stake Sale', Automotive News, 1 March 2019, accessed 20 April 2019, https://www.autonews.com/automakers-suppliers/tata-denies-it-plans-jaguar-land-rover-stake-sale

[79] PR Sanjai, Ruth David, Tommaso Ebhardt and David Welch, 'Tata explores options for struggling Jaguar Land Rover', Bloomberg, 1 March 2019, accessed 20 April 2019, https://www.bloomberg.com/news/articles/2019-03-01/tata-is-said-to-explore-options-for-struggling-jaguar-land-rover

continue to be upset at the ambitious targets they have been handed. They claim to have been forced to sell their cars at a loss, only to meet goals or be able to stock the vehicles in their showrooms.[80]

TATA STEEL'S TAKEOVER OF CORUS

The Corus Group was formed in 1999 after the merger of British Steel and Koninklijke Hoogovens, a Dutch steel producer.[81] This Anglo-Dutch merger aimed at reviving the fortunes of loss-making British Steel, which had lost £81 million in the year ended 31 March 1999.[82] However, it had faced upsets right from the start. Market observers attributed the company's problems to the absence of able leadership, lack of interdepartmental communication, low morale and unrest in the labour force, poor productivity and mismatch between the two cultures, Dutch and British. The unit also suffered from severe technological problems.

When Corus was formed after the merger, the Dutch operations received heavy investments. It soon became a world-

---

[80] *The Economist*, 'Tata to the rescue', *The Economist*, 16 February 2019, accessed 20 April 2019, https://www.economist.com/business/2019/02/16/jaguar-land-rover-is-in-a-hole-mostly-of-its-own-making

[81] Ishita Ayan Dutt, 'Tata-Corus: A merger of inconvenience', *Business Standard*, 31 March 2016, accessed 24 April 2019, https://www.business-standard.com/article/companies/tata-corus-a-merger-of-inconvenience-116033100044_1.html

[82] Rediff.com, 'Why the Tata-Corus merger was doomed to fail', 31 March 2016, accessed 25 May 2019, https://www.rediff.com/money/report/why-the-tata-corus-merger-was-doomed-to-fail/20160331.htm

class unit. But the British Steel operations lagged far behind. This skewed organizational structure was certain to affect the company's financial performance, and it did. The stock market value of Corus fell from $6 billion in 1999 to $230 million in 2003.[83] Corus started hunting frantically for a buyer.

By then, under the leadership of Mr Ratan Tata, growth by acquisitions had become a guiding principle in the operations of Tata Steel. Several incidents in its history had led up to this, perhaps the most notable of which is the case of the Kalinganagar plant in Odisha. Tata Steel had planned this plant as long back as 2004. It faced multiple hurdles—most of them extremely debilitating. A major roadblock was the displacement of villagers. The government had acquired considerable land from the villagers in Kalinganagar for the plant. It was a situation that seemed to be facing constant roadblocks, and most people had written off the project. The Tatas, however, displayed the determination and grit to work with different stakeholders to establish the plant. It was finally inaugurated in November 2015—almost ten years after it had initially been planned.[84]

The Kalinganagar project taught the Tata Group a vital lesson: setting up new ventures in India was risky and complex.

---

[83]Ishita Ayan Dutt, 'Tata-Corus: A merger of inconvenience', *Business Standard*, 31 March 2016, accessed 25 May 2019, https://www.business-standard.com/article/companies/tata-corus-a-merger-of-inconvenience-116033100044_1.html

[84]Bizodisha online, 'Naveen inaugurates Tata's Kalinganagar Steel Plant, asks Co to expand its business in Odisha', 18 November 2015, accessed 25 May 2019, http://bizodisha.com/2015/11/naveen-inaugurates-tatas-kalinganagar-steel-plant-asks-co-to-expand-its-business-in-odisha/

The various permissions that were required, compounded by the bureaucracy and the long-winded process of land acquisition, made any large project time consuming, expensive and prone to delays. To circumvent this situation, the Group started focusing on growing inorganically, i.e., by takeovers and acquisitions. Since the opportunities for acquiring companies domestically in India were limited, the Tatas adopted a global approach and started looking internationally for acquisition targets.[85]

Tata Steel found that a global mindset had another significant advantage: immense value in terms of management practices, product profiles, product mixes and technology for the steel industry.[86] In fact, this realization can also explain the massive influx of suitors for old steel plants that are auctioned off by financial institutions or the courts under bankruptcy acts. These acquisitions are easier to get started up, and much less cumbersome to turn around as compared to setting up greenfield plants in India.

THE DE-INTEGRATION STRATEGY

To bolster the capacities of Tata Steel, the Group followed a de-integration strategy. It involved supplying raw materials

---

[85]Shashank Shah, *The Tata Group: From Torchbearers to Trailblazers*, Penguin Random House India, 2018, Chapter 14
[86]Koushik Chatterjee, CFO Tata Steel in Richard Dobbs and Rajat Gupta, 'An Indian approach to global M&A: An interview with the CFO of Tata Steel', *McKinsey Quarterly*, October 2009, accessed 25 April 2019, https://www.mckinsey.com/business-functions/strategy-and-corporate-finance/our-insights/an-indian-approach-to-global-m-and-38a-an-interview-with-the-cfo-of-tata-steel

and semi-finished materials manufactured from factories in India to finishing facilities that were situated closer to the end consumers.[87] These finishing facilities would also be owned, thereby giving the company a strong foothold in the entire ecosystem.

In kick-starting this strategy, the Tata's first target was Singapore-based NatSteel. In August 2004, the Group acquired NatSteel and added an additional 2 Mtpa capacity (2 million tonnes per annum) to its existing 4 Mtpa capacity in India. The takeover also gave the Tatas access to the surrounding markets in Australia, China, Philippines, Malaysia, Thailand and Vietnam. The Chinese markets were particularly attractive, as the per capita consumption of steel in China was more than six times that of India.[88]

In 2005 the Tatas acquired Millennium Steel, Thailand's largest manufacturer and distributor of long steel products.[89] Over 90 per cent of the sales of Millennium Steel were in the domestic markets. This acquisition added another 1.2 Mtpa capacity to Tata Steel. Eventually in December 2006, the company was renamed to Tata Steel Thailand. The acquisitions

---

[87] Tarun Khanna, Krishna G. Palepu and Richard Bullock, 'House of Tata: Acquiring a Global Footprint', Harvard Business School Case 708-446, May 2008 (Revised June 2009.)

[88] Lavine Quadros and Deepal Shah, 'India Equity Research:Tata Steel', Ask Raymond James and Associates, 1 September 2006, via Thomson Research/Investext, quoted in Tarun Khanna, Krishna G. Palepu and Richard Bullock, 'House of Tata: Acquiring a Global Footprint', Harvard Business School Case 708-446, May 2008 (Revised June 2009.)

[89] https://web.archive.org/web/20130920171449/http://www.tata.in/company/profile.aspx?sectid=bijlJLDdD%2Fo%3D

of NatSteel and Millennium Steel enabled the Tatas to get a distinct edge in the Southeast Asian market. By consolidating the production capacity of these acquisitions, the capacity of Tata Steel almost doubled in two years; after the Corus acquisition Tata Steel saw its global steel rankings rise from fifty-sixth to fifth![90]

It is interesting to dissect the Tata's motivation behind these two acquisitions. Singapore and Thailand were not exactly huge markets back then, but they had a significant population and the Tatas got a presence in seven markets overnight.[91] Also, they were on a rapid growth trajectory and, hence, displayed the potential for becoming attractive markets in the future. These deals also offered the Tatas an opportunity for testing the waters in mergers and acquisitions (M&A) and for learning how to run a transnational business. Mr Koushik Chatterjee, the CFO of Tata Steel at the time, said in an interview that this exercise was almost like a canvas for understanding cultural issues and integrating large organizations.[92]

---

[90]Bloomberg, 'Tata Steel unit buys Vietnam's largest steel mills', LiveMint, 8 March, 2007, accessed 26 May2019, https://www.livemint.com/Companies/dFwCrhAHBXjB4OXJO88t4N/Tata-Steel-unit-buys-Vietnams-largest-steel-mills.html

[91]Eric Bellman, 'Tata Steel to buy NatSteel Assets for $285 million', *The Wall Street Journal*, 16 August 2004, accessed 26 May 2019, https://www.wsj.com/articles/SB109265121682692283

[92]Koushik Chatterjee, CFO Tata Steel in Richard Dobbs and Rajat Gupta, 'An Indian approach to global M&A: An interview with the CFO of Tata Steel', *McKinsey Quarterly*, October 2009, accessed 25 April 2019, https://www.mckinsey.com/business-functions/strategy-and-corporate-finance/our-insights/an-indian-approach-to-global-m-and-38a-an-interview-

THE VERTICAL INTEGRATION STRATEGY

Even back in the 1990s, Tata Steel had its own mines for iron ore and coking coal—raw materials for the steel manufacturing business. It was not dependent on external vendors for its raw material needs. This protected the company from fluctuations in global price movements for these commodities. It was effective vertical integration that helped Tata Steel become one of the lowest-cost steel producers in the world by 2001.[93] (As of 2019, it is the lowest-cost steel producer in Asia.[94])

Tata Steel now started focusing on growth. It began exploring downstream products and commenced the sale of value-added products under its brand name. It became the first Indian steel company to do so. (Downstream products are those products on which some additional processing is done, to take the product one stage closer to the customer. So this would be taking the final products of a firm, and then doing some more processing on it, [or value-addition activities on these products]. Tata Steel made downstream products such as hot rolled, cold rolled and coated steel, rebars, wire rods, tubes and wires.)

It was the year 2006 when the first seeds of the Corus takeover were planted. Mr L.N. Mittal, a steel magnate, acquired Arcelor, a steel manufacturing company based in

---

with-the-cfo-of-tata-steel

[93] Tata Steel Annual 101st report 2007–2008, Message from the Managing Director, accessed 25 April 2019, https://www.tatasteel.com/investors/annual-report-2007-08/html/management_speak.html

[94] Tata steel website, accessed 24 April 2019, https://www.tatasteel.com/corporate/our-value-chain/business-model-strategy/

Luxembourg City, in what was a much-talked-about deal in the business world. At the time, Tata Steel had a capacity of 5 million tonne per annum. The management strongly felt that it needed to have a capacity of at least 25 Mtpa to remain relevant in the industry. After all, the ArcelorMittal merger had created an entity that was the largest in the world—nearly four times larger than the nearest competitor. In this scenario, Tata Steel needed to consider all options for growth, even if they were unprecedented. International acquisitions had to become a core component of the business's growth plan, Mr N. Chandrasekaran, the Tata Steel Chairman at the time, stated later in an interview in 2017.[95]

Mr Ishaat Hussain, Executive Director (Finance), Tata Steel explained the reasons for the Corus takeover as under:

> Mr Mittal has changed the paradigm. There will be global consolidation of steel, and India, because of its inherent competitive advantage in steel, could be one of the entities around which this globalization will take place. You reach a critical mass and perhaps with your own organic growth in India—and Tata Steel will be shouting from the rooftops that all existing plans stand—then organically it will probably go to about 45 million tons. And who knows? It may be another consolidator.
>
> Lakshmi Mittal is one nucleus. We could be the other nucleus. When the day of reckoning came, I just

---

[95] PTI, 'N. Chandrasekaran defends acquisition of Corus Steel', LiveMint, 8 August 2017, accessed 25 April 2019, https://www.livemint.com/Companies/gUAs8jsNykK0TO4n8rqcoI/N-Chandrasekaran-defends-acquisition-of-Corus-Steel.html

sat quietly in my room after the Board meeting and asked myself, 'What would we do without Corus?' We would become a marginal, 10-million-ton steel plant.[96]

Interestingly, Tata Steel wasn't the only company eying Corus; ArcelorMittal and some other companies also explored the option to buy it out. However, Tata Steel appeared to be the only committed bidder. After its two global acquisitions in 2004–06 (that of NatSteel and Millennium Steel), the company had been successful in strengthening its supply chain and gaining access to the Southeast Asian markets. When the opportunity to acquire Corus presented itself, Mr Ratan Tata felt that it was a deal he could not pass up. He stated as much in an interview in 2008:

Corus came to us, we didn't seek them out. In one swoop we were in Europe, where we weren't before... That opportunity was going to happen once, and it was not going to happen again.[97]

Finally, on 5 October 2006, the Tata Group confirmed its interest in Corus. It proposed a cash bid of 455 pence a share.[98] Companhia Siderúrgica Nacional (CSN), a Brazilian

---

[96] Tarun Khanna, Krishna G. Palepu and Richard Bullock, 'House of Tata: Acquiring a Global Footprint', Harvard Business School Case 708-446, May 2008. (Revised June 2009) page 8

[97] Heather Timmons, 'Tata pulls Ford units into its orbit', *The New York Times*, 4 January 2008, accessed 27 April 2019, https://www.nytimes.com/2008/01/04/business/worldbusiness/04tata.html?sq=tata&st=cse&adxnnl=1&scp=7&adxnnlx=1238497443-4R16x3p9Aj5a8CErvf45bw

[98] BS Reporters, 'Tata Corus: Tata bags Corus with 608 pence bid', *Business Standard*, 8 February 2018, accessed 26 May 2019, https://www.business-

steelmaker, also entered the fray and made an offer of 475 pence a share.[99] The Tatas responded with an increased bid of 500 pence, which CSN promptly answered with a raised bid of 515 pence a share. The Corus management decided to take the matter to the Board. Eventually, an auction was conducted to decide the winner.[100] After a seven-hour-long war over eight rounds of bidding, the Tata Group finally emerged victorious. The final bid had been 608 pence a share—a premium of 34 per cent to the original offer. The total payment was $12.1 billion (₹53,580 crore as per the exchange rate at the time).[101] Of this, $6 billion was debt. It seemed like a very expensive acquisition, but the Tatas went through with it because it aligned with their larger vision for Tata Steel.

The Tata-Corus deal made Tata Steel the fifth largest steelmaker[102] in the world with an annual capacity of 25 million tonne. It was, by far, the biggest overseas acquisition any

---

standard.com/article/companies/tata-corus-tata-bags-corus-with-608-pence-bid-107013100044_1.html

[99] Chris Noon, 'Brazil's CSN Tops Tata bid for Corus', *Forbes*, 17 November 2006, accessed 26 May 2019, https://www.forbes.com/2006/11/17/corus-csn-tata-markets-equity-cx_cn_1117markets06.html#7cef61e71698_cn_1117markets06.html#26d3403f1698

[100] Indrajit Gupta, 'Tata Corus: 7 Lessons from a deal from Hell', FoundingFuel, 14 April 2016, accessed 14 April 2019, http://www.foundingfuel.com/column/strategic-intent/tata-corus-7-lessons-from-a-deal-from-hell/

[101] Abhineet Kumar, 'Tata Corus: Crash, crisis and recovery effort', *Business Standard*, 20 January 2013, accessed 26 May 2019, https://www.business-standard.com/article/companies/tata-corus-crash-crisis-and-recovery-effort-112112800063_1.html

[102] ET Bureau, 'Tale of two acquisitions: Mittal Steel's acquisition of Arcelor and Tata Steel's acquisition of Corus', *The Economic Times*, 31 March 2015

Indian company had made until then. The deal gave the Tata Group an instant and major presence in European markets and higher value-added segments such as the construction and automotive sectors. After the acquisition, the management started exploring the merits of extending the de-integrating model to Europe (as had been done for NatSteel and Tata Steel Thailand). Corus, in essence, was not as well integrated as Tata Steel was in India, and this put it at risk when the prices of raw materials and steel fluctuated. Moreover, Corus also had lower margins, which would necessitate that the unit worked extra hard to reduce costs.

In the years that followed, Tata Steel experienced several ups and downs in business. The company had expected the boom in the demand for steel to continue. According to a company presentation made soon after the acquisition, Tata Steel had predicted the global steel demand to grow by 5.9 per cent to 1,179 million tonne in 2007.[103] It had also expected China's and India's steel demand to grow by 13 per cent and 10.2 per cent in the same year. However, contrary to these predictions, the steel prices crashed drastically—from $600 per tonne to less than $400.[104] The supply from China far outstripped the demand from the developed world, and the growth turned negative. Cheap imports from China affected all the emerging markets.

---

[103] Ishita Ayan Dutt, 'European woes test Tata Steel's resilience', *Business Standard*, 18 April 2016, accessed 24 April 2019, https://www.business-standard.com/article/companies/european-woes-test-tata-steel-s-resilience-116041801109_1.html
[104] Ibid.

Corus was also afflicted by other problems. As with JLR, the financial downturn of 2008 impacted Corus too. The company saw multiple changes in the top management. Tata Steel, unfortunately, did not succeed in achieving integration as rapidly as it would have liked to, thereby compounding the challenge. Consequently, Corus, a profit-making company at the time of its acquisition in 2007, lost $303 million in 2010.[105]

In an attempt at rectification, the company undertook job cuts and sale of assets. Tata Steel also sold off some of its assets in the UK. In March 2011, it sold off Teesside Cast Products, an iron and steel plant, to Sahaviriya Steel Industries PCL of Thailand for $467 million. But the losses continued. The Tatas had invested over £1.5 billion in modernizing old plants, but it was estimated that the company was still losing over £1 million per day.[106] The debt-laden company also struggled to improve the performance of its European operations.

Meanwhile, the foreign media was rife with news. The Tatas were, reported the media, considering entering into a joint venture with ThyssenKrupp, the German industrial conglomerate. There were also news stories about the Tatas planning to spin off the Dutch operations along with the UK

---

[105] Abhineet Kumar, 'Tata Corus: Crash, crisis and recovery effort', *Business Standard*, 20 January 2013, accessed 26 May 2019, https://www.business-standard.com/article/companies/tata-corus-crash-crisis-and-recovery-effort-112112800063_1.html

[106] Ishita Ayan Dutt, 'European woes test Tata Steel's resilience', *Business Standard*, 18 April 2016, accessed 24 April 2019, https://www.business-standard.com/article/companies/european-woes-test-tata-steel-s-resilience-116041801109_1.html

plants. These plans, apparently, were stuck because of little clarity on the pension-related liabilities for the employees of Tata Steel UK.

LEARNINGS FROM THE CORUS ACQUISITION

The Tata-Corus deal taught several lessons to the Tata Group—learnings that have come in handy for the business empire's future plans. It is also replete with acquisition tips for business leaders and managers. A media report analysing the takeover summarized some of these learnings[107]:

- Get your timing right: The Tata-Corus deal was made at a time when the commodity cycle was at its peak and the asset prices were high. The steel industry had undergone a massive shift in the cost structures. While earlier, the ratio of the costs of production to the costs of raw material was 70:30, it was now 30:70—an exact opposite! The meaning was clear: the power and the profits had shifted from the steel producers to the miners. This reversal in power had reduced the margins that a company could expect to make from steel production. There was little chance of recovery of the investments.
- Keep emotions out of the bidding process: Some media reports suggest that once CSN, the Brazilian

---

[107] Indrajit Gupta, 'Tata Corus: 7 Lessons from a deal from Hell', Founding Fuel, 14 April 2016, accessed 14 April 2019, http://www.foundingfuel.com/column/strategic-intent/tata-corus-7-lessons-from-a-deal-from-hell/

steelmaker, entered into the bidding process for Corus, the acquisition took on nationalistic overtones. This pushed up the price—possibly beyond what would have been judicious for the Tatas.

- Beware of the auction process: Auctions, in general, can be tricky to tackle. The bids go up in incremental amounts. Since the subsequent increments are usually small, it is easy to overbid unless one is crystal clear about the ceiling one is willing to go to, and sticks to that limit.
- Undertake due diligence: Before going ahead with a takeover, ensure that you perform a proper due diligence on the firm in question. This usually should help you understand the problems that the firm faces and will help you thinking about the possible ways in which you can resolve them, if at all. Also, be clear as to why you need to acquire and the price that you will pay for it.
- One should also use the due diligence to investigate the internal workings of the target company. (In another media report, a former Tata official who worked towards the integration of Corus and Tata admitted: 'When we acquired the company, the fight between the British and Dutch sides was at its peak. We inherited a legacy'.)[108]
- Weigh the merits of cash deals vs. stock buy-outs: The

---

[108]Ishita Ayan Dutt, 'What the Tata Steel write-off reveals', *Business Standard*, 21 May 2013, accessed 16 May 2019, https://www.business-standard.com/article/companies/what-the-tata-steel-write-off-reveals-113052101267_1.html

Corus deal was an all-cash one; the cash came in from borrowed funds. This is a potentially high-risk move. Moreover, the top management of Corus was allowed to liquidate stock options. While this made a lot of them very wealthy, they were, quite possibly, not as invested in the business as they had been before.

- Consider the changing industry dynamics: At the time of the deal, the industry was witnessing widespread transformation. As we already discussed, it was the peak of the commodity cycle, which pushed up the asset prices. Further, the UK steel plant was looking to source its coal from Mozambique and iron ore from Brazil. These plans, however, ran into unexpected hurdles. The high ash content in the coal from Mozambique and the steep prices of the Brazilian ore made it difficult to rely on these sources and hence, this plan could not work.
- Tata Steel's troubles were further compounded by the high cost of power in the UK. The steel production process typically uses a lot of power, and this aggravated the already precarious situation, thus pushing up costs. Additionally, the UK plants were highly overmanned, and it was not possible to cut down the size of the labour force due to strong opposition from unions and local politicians.
- Traditionally, the steel plant in the UK had done well, and, when the demand was high, the high prices could be absorbed by the buyers. But in case of falling demand, when there was pressure to reduce prices or risk losing customers to cheaper imports, the plant

could not match the lower price expectations, due to high costs, and soon became uncompetitive.
- Keep an eye on the money: For the Corus deal, the Tatas were paying a high capital cost. The purchase price of the asset was quite steep, especially when considering that it had been valued far less only a few years ago. Plus, the Group was forced to bid in an auction, which frequently results in increased prices for the buyer. The eventual deal was solemnized using borrowed funds, which was an additional factor in increasing the costs. Possibly, it wasn't as money-wise a deal as it could have been.

WAS THE ACQUISITION OF CORUS A MISTAKE?

The Tata's acquisition of Corus will probably be discussed in business schools around the world for years to come. It has come to be known as one of Tata's biggest disappointments, with several experts recommending exactly what the Group could have done differently. So, was the deal really a mistake? Let us examine this.

Around the time of the Corus acquisition, Tata Steel was growing fast. However, it had reached its peak in India, as the local environment made it difficult for it to grow organically. Every new project was prone to delays and continuous battles with various stakeholders, all of which led to cost and time overruns. Tata Steel needed to explore a different path to achieve growth. It decided to go ahead with the path of acquisitions.

However, India did not present many acquisition targets that could be bought out to an advantage. The Tatas were already struggling with various political and bureaucratic permissions for its existing projects. Another major limitation was that any local venture would need to be of a particular size for it to be economically viable. In fact, new ventures in traditional sectors were difficult even for a group as large and resourceful as the Tatas. Some market analysts also argue that since the Tatas insisted on maintaining their values and ethics (see Chapter 3), they were unwilling to make compromises or pay bribes to get their work done faster. This would also serve as a potential handicap for growth. In this context, the Tatas were left with only one route to expansion: tapping the international markets.

On the international front, Tata Steel had so far followed a smart strategy of de-integration. They served global markets by making low-cost products in their plants at home, at the lowest costs. These semi-finished materials were then shipped to be sold as value-added products to locations that were closer to the end customers. This strategy enabled the firm to get higher margins. It is actually a variant of a similar strategy that is employed by some other business houses, specifically the Kalyani Group. Bharat Forge Limited, the flagship of the Kalyani Group, follows the 'dual shore' strategy, wherein their home-based plants make most of the low-cost production and these are then supplied to high-value markets.[109] This permits

---

[109] R Jagannathan, 'Bharat Forge's dual shore strategy is paying off', DNA India, 22 September 2005, accessed 26 May 2019, https://www.dnaindia.com/business/report-bharat-forge-s-dual-shore-strategy-is-paying-

the company to leverage its low-cost advantage. Of course, this strategy can be successful only when there is an implicit assumption: the quality standards remain the same and the cost of shipping the goods from the base does not exceed the savings from manufacturing in India.

While the Tatas had mastered their strategy, the Corus acquisition suffered the disadvantage of tumultuous market changes after the acquisition. This made it difficult for the deal to pay off in the calculated time period. The high acquisition costs, stiff operating costs and the inability to reduce the labour costs also made things difficult for the Tatas. Under slightly different conditions, perhaps, the acquisition of Corus could have had a better outcome than what actually played out. While the argument about whether or not the takeover was a mistake will continue, the attempts that the Tatas have been making to correct the situation are valuable lessons in themselves.

THE TETLEY ACQUISITION

In 1995, Tata Tea sought to acquire Tetley, a UK-based global tea company, and proposed a bid of ₹1,500 crore. However, the bid failed due to the inability to make timely financial arrangements. In 2000, however, when Tetley came up for sale again, the Tatas were luckier. Their bid was now up to £271 million (₹1,900 crore).[110] They won it in February 2000

---

off-2949

[110] Shashank Shah, 'How India's Tata Tea ended up in English homes', Quartz India, 27 November 2018, accessed 26 May 2019, https://qz.com/

in what was the largest-ever Indian acquisition until then.

The Tetley takeover was the Tata Group's first international acquisition and the largest cross-border takeover ever by an Indian company. Tata Tea was a third of the size of Tetley. In winning the bid, it had overcome competition from Sara Lee, the US consumer products major and Nestle, the Swiss foods major. The acquisition helped Tata Tea become the world's second largest tea company,[111] with sales in forty-four countries. Interestingly, the acquisition was financed mainly by equity of £70 million and the balance was debt.[112] Therefore, Tetley continued to function as a mostly 'independent' company where Tata Tea played a monitoring role. The debt limited the actions that Tata Tea could take in the operations of Tetley, and it remained an advisor until the debt was paid off two years later. Eventually, both Tata Tea and Tata Sons raised their stakes in Tetley, retired the high-cost debt, and integrated the operations to enjoy the full benefits in the areas of tea buying and blending.

The Tetley takeover resulted in multiple gains for Tata Tea. The company graduated from being a primary producer of bulk tea to a producer and marketer of value-added

---

india/1474335/tea-gardens-to-tetley-a-brief-history-of-indias-tata-tea/

[111]Sarath Chelluri, 'Tata Tea: world's second largest branded tea player', *Business Standard*, 29 January 2013, accessed 26 May 2019, https://www.business-standard.com/article/markets/tata-tea-world-s-second-largest-branded-tea-player-108120101031_1.html

[112]Savio G Pinto, 'Tetley Takeover costs Tata Tea 400 million pound', 26 February 2013, accessed 26 May 2019, https://www.business-standard.com/article/specials/tetley-takeover-costs-tata-tea-400-million-pound-100082301012_1.html

branded tea products, including the extremely profitable packet-tea business. As the second largest tea brand in the world, Tetley had sales in forty-four countries, besides being the market leader in the UK and Canada. It also had the second largest market share in the United States. The acquisition, therefore, made Tata Tea a force to reckon with in the global arena. It became the second largest player in the global tea market after Unilever. By 2016, Euromonitor, a market research company data showed that Tata Global Beverages had a market share of 29 per cent in the Indian packet tea market. This was followed closely by Hindustan Lever's (HLL's) share of 27 per cent.[113]

TAKEAWAY

The integration of the acquired company with that of the acquirer is the most crucial element of any acquisition. The Tata Group has exemplified the right way to do this by learning from each of its purchases. Many of these learnings have emanated from the company being bought. Let us summarize the takeaways to keep in mind when exploring the acquisition path for business growth:

- Acquire to add strategic value. Every acquisition must add value to the acquirer and should not be undertaken

---

[113]Richa Maheshwari, 'Now, more Indians prefer small tea brands like Wagh Barki, Amar Tea', *The Economic Times*, 22 June 2017, accessed 26 May 2019, https://economictimes.indiatimes.com/industry/cons-products/food/now-more-indians-prefer-to-have-tea-with-small-brands-like-wagh-bakri-amar-tea/articleshow/59260789.cms?from=mdr

for any other reason.
- Aim to partner, not just acquire.
- Share business activities.
- Continuity of management can often turn out to be effective in implementing rapid but effective integration.
- Learn from the acquirer. Incorporate best practices wherever relevant.
- Don't fall into the price trap but understand where steep prices may be essential to win global scales. For instance, during the planned acquisition of CGP, a UK-based chemicals company, Mr R Mukundan, the Managing Director and CEO of Tata Chemicals, walked away from the negotiations. The prices had exceeded the mental benchmark he had decided for the deal. However, during the Corus acquisition in 1994, the Tatas paid a premium for a takeover they assessed essential for growth.

Mr R. Gopalakrishnan, the Tata Group's executive director as of 2019, encapsulates the above guidelines well:

> When we acquire a company, we do not go in like conquerors. We go in with a collaborative mind-set and seek alignment in terms of our values.[114]

The Group believes that the important thing while planning an acquisition is to keep a sharp lookout for three tests: whether

---

[114]Prashant Kale, Harbir Singh and Anand Raman, 'Don't Integrate your Acquisitions, Partner with them', *Harvard Business Review*, December 2009, accessed April 2019, https://hbr.org/2009/12/dont-integrate-your-acquisitions-partner-with-them

the resulting entity would be better off in the market, how the pricing will be and how effective the deal would be in the backdrop of the prevalent industry structure. It is this approach that has helped the Tata Group make a success out of its acquisitions, even when some of the deals haven't reaped the kind of results that were originally predicted.

9

DISCARD RIGID MANAGEMENT STYLES: HOW TO DEVELOP ENVIRONMENTAL FLEXIBILITY

DON'T STICK TO A MANAGEMENT STYLE, NO MATTER HOW SUCCESSFUL IT HAS BEEN IN THE PAST, IF YOU DON'T THINK IT WOULD FIT THE PRESENT CIRCUMSTANCES.

The Tata Group has witnessed several upheavals in management styles, triggered especially by changes in the top leadership. The Group's ability to make and adapt to such changes, despite its large size and deep presence, is a behaviour that modern businesses should imitate. The best example of developing a management style aligned to changing environmental realities lies in the varying approach to leadership displayed by two of the chairmen: Mr J.R.D. Tata and Mr Ratan Tata.

In 1938, when Mr J.R.D. Tata was elected the chairman

of Tata Sons, the Tata Group comprised fourteen companies. Incidentally, he was at the helm of affairs at the time of the nationalization of the Tata businesses, including Tata Airlines, which was nationalized in 1953 (to Air India and Air India International), and New India Assurance Company Limited, Tata's insurance arm, which was nationalized in 1973.[115]

The Group chairman was usually handpicked by the top management that included Mr Darbari Seth, Chairman, Tata Chemicals and Mr Ajit Kerkar, Chairman, Indian Hotels. But the dismantling of the managing agency system in 1970 by the Indira Gandhi government meant that the Tata companies had become legally independent. Each company now had to run independently with a separate board of directors and a managing director. The new structure was rolled out. However, the companies were still tightly held together by Mr J.R.D. Tata. His charismatic personality, the inter-corporate shareholding ownership network and weekly cross-company directors' meetings did a terrific job of keeping the separate companies functioning as a single unit.[116]

With time, however, this structure changed. Mr J.R.D. Tata started encouraging the chairpersons to work independently and expand and operate their companies within the Tata philosophy of professionalism and ethical business practices. Mr J.R.D. Tata confessed in R.M. Lala's book:

---

[115]https://www.business-standard.com/company/new-india-assura-12214/information/company-history, accessed May 2019
[116]Bakhtiar Dadabhoy, *Jeh: A life of JRD Tata*, Rupa Publications, India, 2005, page 291

> Today, except in Tata Sons, I do not wield any kind of executive authority. But because I am senior in age, I operate more on the basis of influence and confidence.[117]

Mr J.R.D. Tata also rolled out another significant change in the management style: he allowed the dilution of the shareholding of Tata Sons' stakes in the Tata Group companies. This dilution achieved a vital purpose for the Tata Group: it helped the Tatas avoid the limitations of the Monopolies and Restrictive Trade Practices Act, 1969. This Act was passed by the Government of India to restrict the power of large business groups. The Tatas circumvented the restrictive provisions of this Act by rightfully claiming that their companies were independent and professionally managed, with Mr J.R.D. Tata only acting as a part-time chairman.

While the dilution was a well-thought strategy, it *did* sometimes border on being excessively severe. Tata Sons ended up holding only very small stakes in the various Tata companies. In fact, so low were the shareholdings that, at one point, Mr G.D. Birla, a prominent businessman in the Birla Group, held a 5 per cent stake in Tata Steel as compared to the Tata's 3 per cent. This scenario throws light on the good business relations between Mr J.R.D. Tata and Mr G.D. Birla—a rapport that was further extended between Mr Ratan Tata and Mr Kumar Mangalam Birla, Chairman, Birla Group as well.

The media, understandably, questioned the situation.

---

[117]R.M. Lala, *The Creation of Wealth*, Penguin Random House India Private Limited, Kindle edition, Chapter 18

Some newspaper reports stated that the Birlas were planning to sell their stakes in Tata Steel; these rumours were quelled in subsequent reports.[118] It was only when Mr Ratan Tata assumed the chairmanship that the situation was corrected; he had been concerned about it even before he assumed the reins.

Mr J.R.D. Tata's management style of empowering managers stemmed from his astute understanding of people. He firmly believed in letting capable leaders handle their affairs as long as it led to overall gains for the business empire. This is evident from his interview to R.M. Lala:[119]

> With each man I have my own way. I am one who will make full allowance for a man's character and idiosyncrasies. You have to adapt yourself to their ways and deal accordingly and draw out the best in each man.

He added that one of the qualities of leadership is assessing the needs to get the best results for an enterprise. And that he was an active executive Chairman in Air-India as that was the need then. But if one knows that your MD likes to be alone and will get the results that way, it requires suppressing yourself even if painful. 'To lead men, you have to lead them

---

[118] Reeba Zachariah, 'Birlas to offload stake in Tata Steel', *The Times of India*, 13 March 2006, accessed 23 April 2019, https://timesofindia.indiatimes.com/business/india-business/Birlas-to-offload-stake-in-Tata-Steel/articleshow/1448382.cms

[119] R.M. Lala, *The joy of achievement: conversations with JRD Tata*, Penguin, India, 2000. R.M. Lala, 'The Business ethics of JRD Tata', *The Hindu*, 29 July 2004, accessed 26 May 2019, https://www.thehindu.com/2004/07/29/stories/2004072905951200.htm

with affection,' he said.

The business environment in India slowly underwent a change. However, as the Tata companies were being run by loyal technocrats handpicked by Mr J.R.D. Tata, he did not rush to change the existing organizational or managerial structure.[120] This was a situation that simmered over time and made the need for complete upheaval imperative.

Slowly, the perceived power of Mr J.R.D. Tata waned. The culture of independence blew somewhat out of proportion, with the chairmen of the larger companies used to running their 'empires' without interference. While these companies still operated under the Tata brand name, they enjoyed their freedom. The heads grew overprotective of their domains. The situation got so skewed that many of these independent companies did not see any benefit in collaborating, preferring to function in tight silos. Some of the powerful leaders of these times were Mr Darbari Seth, who built Tata Chemicals and Tata Tea; Mr Ajit Kerkar, the force behind the success of Indian Hotels; Mr Russi Mody, the Chairman of Tata Steel; Mr Nani Palkhivala, the Chairman of ACC Ltd and Mr Sumant Moolgaokar, credited to be the architect of Tata Motors.

Understandably, this was one of the first things that Mr Ratan Tata changed when he took over in 1992. The powerful clique of leaders was phased out slowly with Mr Mody's departure in 1993, fuelled by disagreements within the company. In 1997, Mr Palkhivala quit on the grounds of

---

[120]Bakhtiar Dadabhoy, *Jeh: A life of JRD*, Rupa Publications, India, 2005, page 291

health reasons, while Mr Darbari Seth retired in 1995.[121] Mr Ajit Kerkar also retired in 1997, in line with the new retirement policy launched by Mr Ratan Tata putting a cap on the age limits for chairmen positions within the Tata Group. The management style within the Tata Group had now undergone a complete 360-degree change.

TAKEAWAY

The changes in management styles that the Tata Group has experienced are tumultuous in nature. It would be expected, given the size of the Group. While Mr J.R.D. Tata advocated a relatively 'free rein', choosing to believe in the individual managers and giving them tremendous freedom to operate, his successor, Mr Ratan Tata, had a diametrically different approach.

The relatively 'laissez-faire' leadership approach worked well for Mr J.R.D. Tata in the backdrop of the business environment during his tenure. It contributed tremendously to building the capacities and potential of the chosen management executives, most of who performed spectacularly. But after he stepped down, it was a challenge for Mr Ratan Tata to step into his predecessor's shoes and exercise the same sense of control over the now highly independent companies and the need for these companies to be integrated into the Group and

---

[121] Mumbai Correspondent, 'Darbari Seth Dies after Heart Attack in London', *The Telegraph*, 8 December 1999, accessed May 2019, https://www.telegraphindia.com/business/darbari-seth-dies-after-heart-attack-in-london/cid/907680

not operate as isolated entities.

When companies change hands, it is possible that the executives may not develop the same respect and confidence in their new leader. This is a difficult challenge, particularly in established businesses with several veterans. It is probable that Mr Ratan Tata also faced this challenge when he assumed the role of the chairman. The decision to change the management style could have then been a combined result of the changing environment and the imminent need to hold the Group together as Mr J.R.D. Tata had done.

The ground rule is simple: business leaders must be ready to accept the challenge for transformation, no matter what the trigger. They must not hesitate in introducing a much-needed change only to preserve the status quo. As Mr Ratan Tata puts it:

> A life without excitement, ups and downs, is too (much) boring and dull. You need to be a storyteller to your grandchildren, why don't prepare for that from now? We get this life only once; experience every aspect of it. No one ever has grown without falling once. Fail as many times as you can, then only you can succeed. So, quit complaining and start exploring![122]

---

[122] *The Economic Times*, 'On Ratan Tata's 80th Birthday, Some Life Lessons From The Man Himself', *The Economic Times*, 28 December 2017, accessed April 2019, https://economictimes.indiatimes.com/magazines/panache/on-ratan-tatas-80th-birthday-some-life-lessons-from-the-man-himself/dont-miss-the-big-picture/slideshow/62279220.cms

10
HUMILITY IS IMPERATIVE FOR BUSINESS SUCCESS

ADOPT HUMILITY AS A CORE INTERPERSONAL AND PROFESSIONAL VALUE; IT CAN REAP SURPRISING REWARDS.

The Tata Group enjoys an enviable reputation as an upright and transparent business empire invested in the social and economic development of India. Besides this, the Tatas are also renowned for their humility. The Group has consistently had humble leaders leading by example, and the media has never tired of applauding the Group's foothold in humility despite its phenomenal successes. Multiple anecdotes abound on the simple lives that the Tata Group chairmen lead—a lifestyle that extends to their professional space as well.

MR RATAN TATA'S ASCENT TO GROUP CHAIRMAN

While humility may come across as an interpersonal virtue, it also reaps substantial rewards for business development and growth. Let us study the example of Mr Ratan Tata who, before being announced as the next Group chairman, maintained an extremely low profile in the organization.

Mr Ratan Tata was an integral part of the Tata Group much before he became the chairman. However, he was always humble; he maintained a low-key profile. When Mr J.R.D. Tata announced his name as the next chairman, many doubted his ability to lead a group as huge as the Tatas. This unsettled sentiment is something that even Mr Ratan Tata has since acknowledged.

At the time, some business circles eagerly discussed how Mr Ratan Tata's candidature as the Group chairman was fuelled more by luck and less as a predetermined plan. Many had expected that Mr Russi Mody, a capable executive who headed Tata Steel at the time, would be announced the next chairman. After all, Mr Mody enjoyed the trust of Mr J.R.D. Tata—something that insiders were confident would lead him to the next higher position of the Group chairman.

In 1988, Mr J.R.D. Tata asked Mr Russi Mody to take on the additional charge of Tata Motors, which was then headed by Mr Sumant Moolgaokar. This, however, never materialized. Some newspaper reports suggested that Mr Russi Mody had publicly spoken against some Tata leaders and also gone against Tata Motors in the press. Following this, Mr Sumant Moolgaokar refused to hand over the charge to him. Mr Nani Palkivala, a Tata director and eminent jurist, was also considered for the role of the Group chairman. But Mr Palkivala's political views worked against him. Finally,

Mr J.R.D. Tata picked Mr Ratan Tata for the position, despite his low profile in the company at the time. It was a classic example of humility winning the day, proving that mettle and potential can speak for themselves.

PARTNERING WITH EXPERTS: TATA GROUP & JARDINE MATHESON

A consistent approach of the Tata Group has been to partner with the best companies globally in the corresponding industry for most of its new ventures. The Group has not hesitated from venturing into unexplored areas; instead, it has compensated for any lack of expertise by entering into partnership agreements with companies that are the best in the business. The openness to accepting one's weaknesses and approaching partners who can provide the necessary strength have been key factors in the Tata's success.

In 2002, Mr Ratan Tata initiated a sale of 20 per cent stakes in Tata International Limited (TIL) to Jardine Matheson, a Hong Kong-based conglomerate, for ₹1.26 billion. Jardine Matheson, an influential business entity with a presence throughout Asia, wanted to enter India. Partnering with the Tatas seemed to be a good opportunity for the firm.[123]

Under the terms of the sale, Jardine Matheson would not receive a dividend for the next five years. However, it would have the same rights as other Tata companies, i.e., to be on the TIL Board, be involved in the planning of projects and have the

---

[123] Tarun Khanna, Krishna G. Palepu and Danielle Melito Wu, 'House of Tata-1995: The next generation (A),' Harvard Business School Case, 16 February 1998, Case no. 798037

option to invest in new projects where TIL was the promoter.[124]

Mr Ratan Tata's rationale behind the stake sale was straightforward: he planned to use the funds for new ventures promoted by TIL. He also predicted that Jardine Matheson's expertise would come in handy in various businesses, including retailing and distribution, real estate, hotels, engineering, construction and financial services.

While the Tata Group understood the power of partnerships in winning over the market, it did falter in certain areas. For example, the initial sales of the TELCO-assembled Mercedes-Benz E220 cars turned out to be 50 per cent off the initial projections.[125] Mr Ratan Tata admitted that the joint venture had failed to correctly understand the market. It is possible that errors in judgement like these stemmed from an inadequate understanding of changing consumer demands—something that the Group has since focused on with renewed commitment. A Jardine Matheson associate stated in an interview:

> (Mr Ratan Tata is) a careful planner and thinker, and his long-term decisions seem to be spot-on. But he's not good when consumer demand patterns change rapidly.[126]

---

[124]Tarun Khanna, Krishna G. Palepu and Danielle Melito Wu, 'House of Tata-1995: The next generation (A),' Harvard Business School Case, 16 February 1998, Case no. 798037

[125]Cesar Bacani and Shirish Nadkarni, 'The Tata Emperor', Asiaweek.com, 24 January 1997, accessed 14 May 2019, http://edition.cnn.com/ASIANOW/asiaweek/97/0124/biz1.html

[126]Vijay Baoney of Jardine Fleming quoted in Cesar Bacani and Shirish Nadkarni, 'The Tata Emperor', Asiaweek.com, 24 January 1997, accessed 14 May 2019, http://edition.cnn.com/ASIANOW/asiaweek/97/0124/

TAKEAWAY

Today, demonstrating that one is living a simple life has become almost fashionable in most business circles—at least for shaping public perceptions if not in reality. However, the Tata Group believed in and embraced simplicity at all times, even when it was not fashionable to do so, preferring to keep a low profile and grounded approach to business over a more ostentatious style. The managers handling the Group's affairs and the leaders overseeing the business remained committed to humility as a conscious practice and an integral part of how they chose to lead their lives.

The Tatas have also developed competent partnerships with companies that have the expertise and the skills required to become the best in the industry. Entering into profitable partnerships is an excellent business strategy that also draws its origins from acceptance of the need for working together with experts, in areas where one may not have the required experience or expertise.

Humility is an approach that has helped the Group remain grounded and be mindful of changing circumstances. For business leaders, having your head in the clouds or being arrogant of your success can be dangerous, as it blinds you to the many challenges that could be looming in the future. In fact, most great leaders have been humble, and the Tatas exemplify this trait to a T.

biz1.html

11
TAKING OVER IN STYLE: THE J.R.D.-RATAN TATA DYNAMICS

A PLANNED SUCCESSION CAN DETERMINE THE SUCCESS OF YOUR BUSINESS; ENSURE THAT YOUR SUCCESSORS ARE CAPABLE LEADERS AND GIVE THEM A FREE REIN.

The Tata Group has seen several leaders, with many successors bringing with them original thought and different approaches towards business (see Annexure 2). Particularly fascinating is the wave of change that Mr Ratan Tata brought within the Group after taking over the reins from Mr J.R.D. Tata. This succession has some important management lessons for business leaders.

In 1962, Mr Ratan Tata had to return to India. He had been studying architecture at Cornell University. Mr J.R.D. Tata invited him to join the Tatas. One of his earliest responsibilities was to turn around NELCO, which was then the largest manufacturer of radios in India. Yet, its market share was less than

3 per cent. To Mr Ratan Tata's credit, he did succeed in turning around the company; it soon managed to acquire a 20 per cent market share![127] However, the company was shut down due to a labour union strike and subsequent lockout. Subsequently, Mr Ratan Tata was handed over the ropes of Empress Mills, another troubled company within the Group (It was registered in Bombay in 1874 in the name of Central India Spinning, Weaving, and Manufacturing Company Limited[128]). He achieved a turnaround here too, making the company profitable. In fact, it soon started declaring dividends.

Eventually, when Mr Ratan Tata was given the management of Central India Mills (also popularly known as Empress Mills) in Nagpur, he decided that a modernization plan would need to be rolled out to make the company profitable and competitive. However, his plans met with a roadblock: opposition from the Board. The opposition was led by Mr Nani Palkhivala, who felt that instead of investing further in the company, the Tata Group should exit the business. Mr Palkhivala felt that the Indian textile industry was not doing well.[129] The Board did not sanction the sum of ₹50 lakh that Mr Ratan Tata had

---

[127] Amrita Nair Ghaswalla, 'The Importance of Failure', *The Hindu BusinessLine*, 27 December 2012, accessed 27 May 2019, https://www.thehindubusinessline.com/news/variety/The-importance-of-failure/article20545477.ece

[128] Rachna Tyagi, 'Tata Group history is also the history of Indian industry', *The Week*, 14 October 2018, accessed 27 May 2019, https://www.theweek.in/theweek/cover/2018/10/05/tata-group-history-is-also-the-history-of-indian-industry.html

[129] Vir Sanghvi.com, interview with Ratan Tata on 24 July 2005, http://www.virsanghvi.com/People-Detail.aspx?Key=3, accessed 25 April 2019

wanted to invest towards the modernization. The company was also affected by the Mumbai Textile workers strike led by Datta Samant, and was finally closed in 1986.[130]

Mr Ratan Tata assessed that the Tata Group needed a strategic plan if it was to maintain its growth in the future. Keeping the instances of NELCO and Central India Mills in mind, he wrote a letter to Mr J.R.D. Tata in May 1978.[131] The letter stemmed from his concern that the Group might disintegrate—a situation that concerned him as a member of the Tata Sons Board. This letter subsequently became the basis for the 'Tata Plan'.

The contents of the letter focused essentially on the Tata Group's strategy for the future. Five or ten years in the future, would the Tatas operate as a single unified group or a loosely connected group of independent companies? If the Tatas were to operate as a group, wrote Mr Ratan Tata, then 'several strategic decisions need to be taken relating to the projected organizational and operational structure of the Tatas'.[132]

In his letter, Mr Ratan Tata outlined three steps that he believed would help to formulate a concrete action plan:[133]

1. To provide a long-term direction for existing and

---

[130]Aveek Datta, 'Ratan Tata: A journey in four stages', LiveMint, 28 December 2012, accessed 27 May 2019, https://www.livemint.com/Companies/n47iePUboPWvCqG5FM8IVK/Ratan-Tata-A-journey-in-four-stages.html

[131]Ratan Tata interview, http://tata.com/media/interviews/inside.aspx?artid=+aChutu5R14=

[132]R.M. Lala, *The Creation of Wealth*, Penguin Random House India Private Limited, Kindle edition, Chapter 18

[133]Ibid.

future activities, product areas and international operations

2. To set the operating guidelines for all the Group companies by clearly defining the objectives for growth, earnings, technology utilization, R&D, industrial relations and employee benefits

3. To adopt the necessary group structure which would best meet these objectives (This would include steps such as grouping companies in related businesses, separating or divesting unrelated or loss-making businesses, and creating new corporate entities for new lines of business.)

Mr Ratan Tata's letter revealed his clarity of thought as well as the urgency with which the Tatas would have to operate if they wished to be competitive in the changing environment. In a newspaper interview with the *Financial Times* in 2005, Mr Ratan Tata commented on the 'horrifying situation' that he had to face, at the time he took over the chairmanship. He felt that the Tatas were an empire only in name; powerful executives ruled the operating companies and only paid 'lip-service' to the Group. The Board was filled with elderly dignitaries, some of whom allegedly fell asleep during meetings.[134]

---

[134] Andrew Gowers and Krishna Guha, 'Giant steps for a giant colossus', *Financial Times*, 2 August 2005, accessed 24 April 2019, https://www.ft.com/content/89563062-037c-11da-b54a-00000e2511c8

POST THE TAKEOVER

After becoming the Group chairman, Mr Ratan Tata immediately got to work and took the following steps:[135]

1. Regain control of the operating companies: In 1991–98, Mr Ratan Tata engaged in a series of tough battles with the existing management to regain management control of the main Tata companies.
2. Consolidate the Group shareholdings: Starting in 1991, Mr Ratan Tata used the earnings from the extremely profitable TCS to increase the Group shareholding to 26 per cent.
3. Invest heavily in modernization and upgradation: Mid-1990s onwards, Mr Ratan Tata encouraged the bigger Tata companies to invest heavily in modernizing and upgrading antiquated plant and equipment.
4. Globalization: Beginning in 2001, Mr Ratan Tata encouraged the Tata companies to look beyond India and acquire foreign companies where relevant. This would prove instrumental in obtaining the brands, scale, customers and international networks that were vital for successful operations in a global economy.
5. Divest businesses that underperform: Mr Ratan Tata also proposed to sell off or close down underperforming businesses. However, this proposal ran into some resistance within the Group. It is possible that this was triggered by

---

[135] Andrew Gowers and Krishna Guha, 'Giant steps for a giant colossus', *Financial Times*, 2 August 2005, accessed 24 April 2019, https://www.ft.com/content/89563062-037c-11da-b54a-00000e2511c8

the prevailing sentiment among many employees of the Group, who believed that the Tata staff were committed (and employed) for a lifetime. Mr Ratan Tata had already faced a great backlash when he had sold TOMCO to HLL—something that he later recalled as scary for a new chairman to face.[136]

6. Build a transition plan for succession: This preparation would ensure that that the firm did not have to face succession-related challenges and that this would be done in a planned manner.
7. Revive the retirement policy: Mr Ratan Tata revived an old retirement policy within the Group that set the retirement age for the executive directors, including the managing directors and executive chairpersons, at 65 years. The retirement age for non-executive directors was set at 75 years. While this policy had already been in place, it had never been enforced (until 1992). This policy also stirred up a lot of resentment, as the incumbent chairmen in many Tata Group companies were close to the preset age and would have to step down.

The somewhat-drastic changes ushered in by Mr Ratan Tata did not go down well with everyone. He had to address considerable opposition to several of his decisions. But he plodded on, driven by faith in the steps he was taking.

In 2002, the Tata Group lowered the retirement age of the

---

[136]James Crabtree, 'Chai with the FT: Ratan Tata', *Financial Times*, 14 December 2012, accessed 24 April 2019, https://www.ft.com/content/1ede394c-437e-11e2-a68c-00144feabdc0

non-executive directors to 70 years (from 75) while retaining that of the executive directors at 65 years. This underwent some changes in the successive years, especially in 2005, when the age limit for the non-executive directors was raised once again to 75 years. Finally, in 2011, Tata Sons finalized the retirement age of the non-executive directors to 70 years.[137] The main purpose of this move was to make the process of succession smooth.

There were some eyebrows raised, when the limit was raised, which also resulted in Mr Ratan Tata extending his tenure. He admitted that since he was in the midst of some organizational changes, he could not hand over the chairmanship before these were finished.

TAKING CALCULATED RISKS

An aspect of management that can become potentially problem-ridden during a takeover is risk-taking. Most successors may be averse to taking risks to avoid any change in the status quo, especially when the company is already doing well. However, Mr Ratan Tata realized that taking calculated and strategic risks would have to be an important part of the Tata's growth story. He defined risk-taking as the ability to do things that had not been done before.[138]

---

[137] Mail Today Bureau, 'Tata Groups cuts retirement age for executive directors', *India Today*, 11 April 2011 accessed 24 April 2019, https://www.indiatoday.in/business/corporate/story/tata-group-cuts-retirement-age-for-executive-directors-132000-2011-04-11

[138] Ratan Tata, quoted in 'Vision of the future' interview with Christabelle Noronha, 11 August 2006, accessed May 2019, http://www.tata.com/0_

Taking Over in Style: The J.R.D.-Ratan Tata Dynamics

Under Mr Ratan Tata, risk-taking became a core part of the Tata's business philosophy. In his opinion, businesses had the option to be risk averse and avoid taking any chances whatsoever. This could lead to growth at a particular, often severely restricted pace. On the other hand, a business could also choose to be prudent and take calculated risks to boost this pace of growth. He felt that while the Tata Group had grown over time, the pace of growth had been slow because of an intrinsic tendency to avoid taking chances.[139] Many of the Group companies refrained from taking risks either because a certain move had never been attempted before or was deemed to be unsafe. They preferred to do things in small incremental steps instead of thinking big. Mr Ratan Tata resolved to remedy this situation, beginning with Tata Steel (TISCO) and Tata Motors (TELCO), both of which were in troubled waters when he took over as the chairman.

TISCO and TELCO had long operated in a closed economy, and this had led to a situation where no one paid much attention to factors such as costs, quality or customer satisfaction. Since these companies made up 50 per cent of the Group turnover, their performance had a tremendous impact on the performance of the Tata Group in entirety.

---

media/features/interviews/20060811_ratan_tata.htm quoted in Tarun Khanna, Krishna G. Palepu and Danielle Melito Wu, 'House of Tata-1995: The next generation (A)', Harvard Business School Case, 16 February 1998, case no.798037

[139] Aveek Datta, 'Ratan Tata: A journey in four stages', LiveMint, 22 December 2012, accessed 24 April 2019, https://www.livemint.com/Companies/n47iePUboPWvCqG5FM8IVK/Ratan-Tata-A-journey-in-four-stages.html

Mr Ratan Tata surmised that he had to step in and take action when TISCO and TELCO announced a drop in their earnings—41 per cent and 77 per cent respectively. He stated in an interview that it was all very well not to intervene when the companies were in good shape, but beleaguered companies had to be turned around to preserve the success of the parent group.[140]

Mr Ratan Tata started investing in technological upgradation and the revamping of products. Tata Motors announced the launch of the Indica, the first passenger vehicle designed in India (see Chapter 4). Under his guidance, the Group renewed its focus on quality and productivity, especially in these two companies, and this led to improved performance. Once these measures had been adopted, TISCO emerged as one of the lowest-cost steelmakers in the world.[141]

Mr Ratan Tata also extended the reach of the Tata Group by entering into joint ventures with multinationals, particularly in the high-tech sector. These included ventures with global giants such as IBM and Mercedes-Benz.

SETTING UP THE GROUP EXECUTIVE OFFICE (GEO)

Another significant transformation that Mr Ratan Tata

---

[140] Cesar Bacani and Shirish Nadkarni, 'The Tata Emperor', Asiaweek.com, accessed 24 April 2019, http://edition.cnn.com/ASIANOW/asiaweek/97/0124/biz1.html

[141] Aveek Datta, 'Ratan Tata: A journey in four stages', LiveMint, 22 December 2012, accessed 24 April 2019, https://www.livemint.com/Companies/n47iePUboPWvCqG5FM8IVK/Ratan-Tata-A-journey-in-four-stages.html

ushered in after taking over as the chairman was the setting up of a GEO. It comprised three new executives and two Tata insiders (usually 'star' executives).

The GEO was a dream team established to augment the restructuring efforts within the Group, oversee new ventures and refocus the Group portfolio from the existing forty-five businesses to fewer, more focused ventures through spinoffs, mergers and divestments. The GEO executives also sat on the Boards of individual Tata companies, thereby increasing the cohesiveness of the member companies with the overall group. Finally, they also had responsibilities in the areas of new business development, finance, strategy, HR development and cross-company initiatives. The GEO soon became a major corporate governance initiative within the Tata Group.[142]

When the GEO was first started, the three external members chosen were Mr Gopalakrishnan from Hindustan Lever (HLL), Unilever's Indian subsidiary; Mr Manab Bose from General Electric (GE) and Mr Kishor Chaukar from Industrial Credit and Investment Corporation of India (ICICI). Mr Gopalakrishnan was advising the Group on the brand initiatives and, in December 1998, set up the Brand Equity Fund.[143] The GEO also developed and executed the Tata BEBP agreement to provide a formal group structure

---

[142] Radhika Dhawan, 'Restructuring for Excellence', *Business Today*, accessed 27 May 2019, http://archives.digitaltoday.in/businesstoday/20000322/cover.html

[143] https://www.sec.gov/Archives/edgar/data/926042/000119312504156777/dex41.htm

and legally bind the various companies within the Group. The basic premise of the agreement was that any company signing it would come to be defined as a Tata Group affiliate.

The GEO proved to be a beneficial construct to build group cohesiveness and substantiate the Tata brand. It also played a role in strengthening Tata Administrative Services (TAS), the Group's dream pool of future managers and leaders. The most significant outcome was a hike in the compensation levels so they could become at par with those in multinational firms.

Subsequently, the GEO was merged with the Group Corporate Center (GCC). In 2016, it was disbanded by Tata Sons.[144]

TAKEAWAY

Mr Ratan Tata had taken over what was a very successful business empire, easily one of the largest in the country. Many of the Group companies were leaders in their respective sectors. There was no direct pressure on him to boost the Group's growth or bring about drastic changes. But Mr Ratan Tata displayed the vision and foresight of realizing that the business environment had changed. He identified that the Tata companies were woefully unprepared to operate in this changed environment, let alone compete or prosper. He was

---

[144]PTI, 'Tata Sons disbands Group Executive Council set up by Cyrus M', 24 October 2016, accessed in April 2019, https://timesofindia.indiatimes.com/business/india-business/Tata-Sons-disbands-Group-Executive-Council-set-up-by-Cyrus-Mistry/articleshow/55036886.cms

quick to understand the need of the hour, willing to act on it and equipped with the leadership skills to turn the situation around in the company's favour. These are skills that a worthy business successor must possess for a succession to be successful.

It is interesting to note how Mr Ratan Tata learnt from mistakes committed by predecessors and former managers and did not allow power centres to form within the Group. He insisted on consolidation, a strictly enforced retirement policy that had to be followed, and transparent governance that would work for the well-being of the overall group as opposed to only specific companies.

Finally, Mr Ratan Tata also possessed the self-confidence to stand up against powerful managers who were well entrenched in their companies. This took a lot of courage, especially for a new chairman who had hitherto always been low key. But it was this courage and determination that propelled the Group towards success and prevented the simmering undercurrents from forming into gigantic deadlocks.

12
TREAD THE UNTRODDEN PATH: THE TATAS & NATION-BUILDING

EXPLORE UNEXPLORED BUSINESSES WITH CONFIDENCE AND BUOYANCY, PREFERRING TO TIE IN BUSINESS VENTURES WITH NATION-BUILDING WHEREVER RELEVANT.

> *If everyone is told not to go into unrelated businesses, how will the airlines, oil, and telecommunications industries develop? The government has said that they can't do it. So there's a social benefit to all this diversification.*
>
> —Mr N.A. Soonawala,
> Director, Tata Sons[145]

---

[145]Tarun Khanna, Krishna G. Palepu and Danielle Melito Wu, 'House of Tata-1995: The next generation (A)', Harvard Business School Case, 16 February 1998, Case no.798037

For a business empire to continue to succeed, it becomes imperative at a certain point to go where no one else may have gone before. Venturing into unrelated or hitherto unexplored businesses is understandably unnerving. However, it can also become the foundation of success, as has been in the case of the Tata Group. Interestingly, the Tatas have brilliantly blended exploratory projects with nation-building, wherein their new ventures are based on concepts and promises that can better the social and economic standing of the country.

During his chairmanship, Mr Ratan Tata steered the Group into several diverse industries and frontiers. He encouraged many projects, some of which necessitated the deep pockets and clout that could be obtained only by partnering with conglomerates. Under his leadership, the Tata Group considered joint ventures with American International Group (AIG), a major player in the insurance world; International Tech Park, Bangalore (ITPB), a Singapore-based consortium for setting up a technology park in Bangalore (the Tata stakes were later acquired by Acendas); SIA and Bell Canada for telecommunications. As a part of his initiative to explore businesses that could contribute to the welfare of the nation, Mr Ratan Tata planned to set up new technology companies through TIL.

THE AVIATION DREAM: TATA GROUP & SIA

One of these plans involved entering into a joint venture with SIA to establish a domestic Indian airline.

In 1995, the Tatas submitted a bid to the Indian

government. The bid was well within the framework of the governmental guidelines at the time. If the joint venture were approved, SIA would hold a 40 per cent stake while the Tata companies would hold another 40 per cent. The shareholding of Indian institutional investors would stand at 20 per cent. The resulting high-profile domestic airline would be a $700-million project in total. After the approvals came in, the Tatas planned to acquire nineteen planes and integrate them into SIA's international network.[146]

The proposed structure stood out in sharp contrast to the prevalent shareholding pattern in India's two major government-owned airlines—Air India and Indian Airlines. Each of these airlines held an equity base of less than ₹1 billion. Also, the fleet that the Tatas intended to build was almost at par with the established, government-owned players in the sector (the Tata-SIA venture would own nineteen planes at a time when Indian Airlines operated twenty-five). It is safe to assume that such a venture would have changed the entire nature of India's airline industry. In fact, Joseph Thachil, an aviation analyst, admitted as much in an interview:

> The airline business needs large amounts of capital. Only a venture with big players such as Tata and SIA could really get a handle on it. They can give Indian Airlines a run for its money.[147]

---

[146]Cesar Bacani and Shirish Nadkarni, 'The Tata Emperor', AsiaWeek.com, accessed 9 May 2019, http://edition.cnn.com/ASIANOW/asiaweek/97/0124/biz1.html
[147]Ibid.

However, the proposed joint venture between TIL and SIA failed to materialize. It required the approvals of the Foreign Investment Promotion Board (FIPB) of the Ministry of Industry as well as the Ministry of Civil Aviation. The Tatas expected that the approvals would come in eventually. However, the Ministry of Civil Aviation was strongly opposed to permitting foreign direct investment (FDI) in the airline industry. It planned to adopt a firm policy to prevent such an occurrence. The reasoning was something that the Tata Group found difficult to contest. Mr C.M. Ibrahim, the Civil Aviation Minister at the time, argued:

> Indian Airlines is the national carrier and we have to protect its interests. Otherwise, the future of thousands of employees working for Indian Airlines will be at stake.[148]

WHY DID THE TATA-SIA PROJECT NEVER SEE DAYLIGHT?

The reasons behind the failed project are up for debate. The rejection could have stemmed from political as well as financial factors. Some believe that the government rejected the application on the fear that Indian Airlines would suffer. Another factor given was that nowhere in the world was a foreign airline allowed to operate in the domestic sector.[149]

---

[148] BSCAL, 'Jet Air To Be Asked To Shed Foreign Stake', *Business Standard*, 27 January 2013, https://www.business-standard.com/article/specials/jet-air-to-be-asked-to-shed-foreign-stake-197010701051_1.html.

[149] Amberish Diwanji, 'Eternity on the runway, as take-off signal remains elusive', Rediff.com, accessed May 27 2019, https://www.rediff.com/

Surprisingly, when Mr H.D. Deve Gowda became the Indian Prime Minister in 1996, he displayed a more sympathetic approach to the proposed Tata-SIA venture. It almost seemed that the project would come through especially after the foreign investment board gave its approval. However, a minister stalled the project. He recommended that the decision be put on hold until the cabinet approved a new aviation policy.[150]

As the situation became more and more complicated and the approvals started to appear more improbable, the disappointment of the Tatas grew. Even more distressing was the implication of the deadlock: it seemed that the government had effectively disallowed any foreign airline to invest in India. However, under the prevalent rules, non-Indians could own up to 40 per cent of a local carrier. In fact, this was the joint share of Kuwait Airways, Gulf Air and an Arab consortium in Jet Airways (one of India's private airlines at the time).

Speaking to *Asia Week* in 1997, Mr Ratan Tata expressed his disappointment and confusion about why the Tata-SIA project had been stalled. He said that he did not know where they stood. Approvals from the FIPB and then the Civil Aviation Ministry to grant a no-objection certificate were needed. Their view was that there is no parking space and counter space at airports, and that the skies are crowded.

---

business/1998/sep/01tata2.htm

[150]Cesar Bacani and Shirish Nadkarni, 'The Tata Emperor', Asiaweek.com, 24 January 1997, accessed 14 May 2019, http://edition.cnn.com/ASIANOW/asiaweek/97/0124/biz1.html

> I've always been a proponent of a totally free market. Even though it would hurt some of our companies, I have not endorsed any kind of restraint or barrier to protect Indian industry.
>
> We have a tremendous role to play in the development of Asia and there are many abroad who feel that India is going to be one of the tigers of the next two decades. But it will never be if we build walls around us.[151]

The Tatas had treated their earlier aviation venture—the now nationalized Air India—exceptionally well. It is widely reported that under Mr J.R.D. Tata, the service of Air India was of very high standards. He would take personal care of the passengers even when he was himself travelling as a passenger. A very hands-on business leader, he would often take notes on things that needed to be fixed in order to improve the performance of the airline further. Even things like the level to which wine was poured into a wine glass to the hairstyle of the airhostesses, to the cleanliness of the airline counters, nothing escaped Mr J.R.D.'s watchful eye. As the chairman of Air India, he devoted over 50 per cent of his time to the airline, even though he did not receive any financial rewards for himself or the other companies within the Tata Group.[152]

Thanks to Mr J.R.D. Tata's high degree of personal involvement, the service standards of Air India attracted

---

[151] Cesar Bacani and Shirish Nadkarni, 'The Tata Emperor', Asiaweek.com, 24 January 1997, accessed 14 May 2019, http://edition.cnn.com/ASIANOW/asiaweek/97/0124/biz1.html

[152] Shashank Shah, *The Tata Group: From Torchbearers to Trailblazers*, Penguin Random House India, 2018

worldwide repute. In fact, in the 1970s, when the Government of Singapore set up SIA to attract tourists to the country, it chose to collaborate with Air India to learn world-class service standards. Air India also became the inspiration for other South Asian carriers such as Cathay Pacific and Thai Airways.

It was during the tenure of the Morarji Desai government (1977–79) that Mr J.R.D. Tata was removed from the chairmanship of Air India, and the directorship of Indian Airlines. This was a month after Air India's first Boeing 747, plunged into the sea off Bombay in January 1978 thus killing all 213 passengers and crew on-board. This was attributed to pilot error, and was regarded as one of the greatest air tragedies of the time.[153] Mr J.R.D. Tata was reappointed on the board of both airlines, in 1980 when Indira Gandhi came back to power, but not as the chairman.

The Tata-SIA proposal for a domestic airline was kept hanging for several years. Eventually, the Tata Group had subsequently been permitted to set up joint ventures with Air Asia and Vistara.

TAKEAWAY

The aviation story was a setback for the Tata Group, especially because the Tatas had been keen to enter the sector not for

---

[153]Shashank Shah, 'How the government took Air India from JRD Tata, asked him to run it, and then took it away again', Scroll.in, 5 December 2018, accessed May 2019, https://scroll.in/article/904431/how-the-government-took-air-india-from-jrd-tata-asked-him-to-run-it-and-then-took-it-away-again

business gains but also for giving a fillip to air travel in India. They had wanted to own an airline ever since Tata Airlines had been nationalized back in 1953.

However, even though the Tata-SIA venture could not see fruition, it does throw light on the Group's willingness to patiently wait for better circumstances to prevail, or the regulations to change.

If business leaders and managers succeed in aligning business plans (especially new business ventures) with the larger good of the country they operate in, the rewards can be enriching. This is truer of large business empires that have the advantage of size or companies that have partners with deep pockets and the required expertise. The Tatas have been at the forefront of promoting projects which have helped in nation-building.

13

CHOOSE YOUR PRIORITIES WISELY: POSITIVE SOCIAL IMPACT VS PROFIT

AIM TO CREATE A POSITIVE IMPACT ON THE SOCIETY IN WHICH YOUR BUSINESS OPERATES. SHARPENING THIS FOCUS ALSO LEADS TO GAINS IN BUSINESS AND BRAND EQUITY.

One of the most challenging responsibilities of a business leader is deciding the focus area of his/her business empire. At the outset, this might seem obvious: doesn't every business exist to earn a profit? However, it is rarely as straightforward as that. For continued and consistent success, it is imperative that any company ascertains its priorities wisely, mastering the delicate balance between earning profits and creating a positive social impact.

In this chapter, we will examine the initiatives that the Tata Group has taken for social upliftment and how they have proved to be instrumental in cementing both its reputation and financial standing.

THE TRUST STRUCTURE

We discussed earlier how the Tata Group has long relied on a Trust-based structure (see Annexure 3). These Trusts, besides leading social welfare activities in India, also laid an early foundation for developing indigenous scientific and technological talent. In 1936, they funded the Tata Institute of Social Sciences (TISS). In 1941, India's first cancer hospital, Tata Memorial Hospital, was established in Mumbai while the Tata Institute of Fundamental Research (TIFR) came up in 1945. At present, there are three main Trusts in the Tata structure, each with a different focus area. Let us study them in some depth to understand their place within the Group:

1. J.N. Tata Endowment Trust (Tata Educational Endowment Fund)

This Trust was set up in 1892 by Mr Jamsetji Tata, the founder of the Tata Group. It aims to motivate youngsters to pursue higher studies at leading global universities. Even back in 1892, Mr Jamsetji Tata issued several grants to promising students, including two female doctors who wished to study overseas and specialize in gynaecology.

The J.N. Tata Endowment Trust adopts a reinvestment philosophy. Mr Tata famously explained the rationale behind this approach: 'I can afford to give, but I prefer to lend.'[154] The idea is that the returns can benefit many other students, thereby continuing the core mission.

---

[154] R.M. Lala, *Beyond the Last Blue Mountain: A life of J.R.D.Tata*, Penguin Random House India, 2017, page 301

The Trust has been instrumental in shaping the careers of many scholars over the decades.

2. Sir Ratan Tata Trust (SRTT)

This was established in 1919 to provide grants across five thematic areas: rural livelihoods and communities, education, health, enhancing civil society and governance, and arts and culture.

3. Sir Dorabji Tata Trust

The third Trust was established in 1932 to fund international cancer research in memory of Sir Dorabji's wife, Lady Meherbai, who died of leukaemia. This Trust today continues to work in collaboration with NGOs across the country. As per their website in 2019, the Sir Dorabji Tata Trust works with over 700 NGOs.[155] The Trusts disburses funds to NGOs working in the fields of health, education, livelihoods, social development and natural resources management.

Mr A.N. Singh, Sir Dorabji Tata Trust managing trustee, explains the rationale behind working with NGOs for positive social impact:[156]

> ...anybody who is anybody in the civil society NGO sector has some association with the Trust. It is through these partners that our money goes far and wide, that it gets extended into the rural countryside and benefits a

---

[155] www.tata.com/ourcommitment/articles/inside.aspx?artid= nMP7URJ8 ZTY=, accessed 4 March 2019
[156] Ibid.

larger number of people.

The idea is that by empowering the NGOS, they help the communities they are involved with, as well as the Tatas.

Interestingly, this Trust has more partners than even the Ford Foundation, an American foundation established by Ford family to advance human welfare. However, it has chosen to adopt a different model that avoids the spotlight.

Recently, the Sir Dorabji Tata Trust underwent a strategic shift in its philanthropy. It decided to focus its energies on specific themes in important areas that were frequently neglected. The idea is to create a 'critical mass' that would help the Trust measure the impact it helped to create. It was also preferable to the widely diffused ideas that otherwise came in from the numerous partners. One of the chosen areas under the new approach is urban poverty. To address this pressing concern, the Trust undertakes several activities such as investing in rural livelihoods, creating local jobs to alleviate migration and promoting industrialization in rural areas. The guiding principle of the Trust is outlined on Tata's corporate website and reproduced below:

> Sir Dorabji Tata put all his wealth, estimated at Rs 10 million, into a Trust for use, 'without any distinction of place, nationality or creed,' for the advancement of learning and research, the relief of distress, and other charitable purposes.[157]

---

[157] Corporate website, http://arch.tata.com/aboutus/articlesinside/In-the-name-of-the-father, accessed 9 May 2019

OFFERING EMPLOYEE BENEFITS

If there is something that truly ties in the members of a business empire and deepens their level of commitment to the organization, it is employee benefits. Offhand, it won't be an exaggeration to say that the Tata Group is one of the best known for providing a myriad of benefits to its employees. This is partly responsible for its societal perception as a nurturing and nourishing employer—an increasing rarity in today's short-term, cost-conscious world. Let us understand how the Tata Group operates in this realm and why its approach deserves to be emulated.

The Tatas offered benefits to their employees even before this was mandated by law. This originated with Mr J.R.D. Tata who, after becoming the Group chairman, was surprised that the Tatas lacked a dedicated department for labour welfare. Mr J.R.D. Tata found it extremely odd that a factory with 30,000 machine tools was certain to have a special person or department to look after these tools, but a workforce of 30,000 people had no one to address their needs and concerns![158] Consequently, Tata Steel became the first company in the world to have a dedicated labour department.

Over the years, Tata Steel rolled out multiple employee benefits for its workforce:

- In 1912, the workers had an eight-hour workday. This was at a time when the British had twelve-hour workdays.[159]

---

[158] Shashank Shah, *The Tata Group: From Torchbearers to Trailblazers*. Penguin Random House India Private Limited, 2018, Kindle edition

[159] Nevin John, 'Rock Solid', *Business Today*, 7 April 2019, accessed 27 May

- In 1915, Tata Steel started a rest house for the women working at the coke ovens. This helped them get some rest and sleep during the day.
- Tata Steel started a crèche on the premises so that the children could be looked after by professional nurses.
- In 1936[160], the company introduced 'Leave with Pay' and a workmen's accident compensation scheme. Both of these were quite unknown in even Britain or America at the time.
- In 1920, a Workers' Provident Fund scheme was launched. Again, this was an unfamiliar concept for the workers in England. Even the Government of India legally established this scheme only in 1945; the British rolled it out even later in 1952.
- Starting from 1928, the company empowered women workers with maternity benefits under the Maternity Benefit Scheme. Contrast this with how the measure became mandatory in Bihar only much later in 1946!

Tata Steel also provided bonuses to workers along with several free facilities, including housing, healthcare and education for the workers' families.

2019, https://www.businesstoday.in/opinion/rock-solid/story/328690.html
[160]Nevin John, 'Rock Solid', *Business Today*, 7 April 2019, accessed 27 May 2019, https://www.businesstoday.in/opinion/rock-solid/story/328690.html

EMPLOYEE BENEFITS ISSUED BY THE TATA GROUP

The table below summarises the early-twentieth-century worker benefits programmes implemented at Tata Sons:[161]

Benefit	Year of Introduction	Mandatory under Indian Law	Legal Measure
Eight-hour workday	1912	1948	Factories Act
Free medical aid	1915	1948	Employees State Insurance Act
Establishment of welfare departments	1917	1948	Factories Act
Schooling facilities for workers' children	1917	–	–
Department to handle worker grievances	1919	1947	Industrial Disputes Act
Leave with pay	1936	1948	Factories Act
Worker's Provident Fund	1920	1952	Employees Provident Fund Act

---

[161] Adapted from R.M. Lala, *The Creation of Wealth*, Penguin-Viking, New Delhi, 2004, pp. 284–85

Workman's Accident Compensation Scheme	1920	1924	Workman's Compensation Act
Technical Training for Apprentices	1921	1961	Apprentices Act
Maternity Leave with Benefits	1928	1946	Bihar Maternity Benefit Act
Profit Sharing Bonuses	1932	1965	Bonus Act
Retirement Gratuity	1937	1972	Payment of Gratuity Act
Ex-Gratia Payment – Road Accidents	1979	–	–

The employee benefits rolled out by the Tatas attracted worldwide repute for the Group. In 1956, when Mr Karesasp Naoroji, the grandson of Dadabhai Naoroji, attended the International Labour Organization Committees on Iron and Steel at Ohio, USA, he spoke in glowing terms about the consideration shown by Tata Steel. This was in response to something rather disparaging stated by one of the American speakers—the perception was that Indian workers worked as if on bonded labour. As a representative of the Employers Federation of India, Mr Karesasp Naoroji discussed his experiences as Tata Steel employee and how the workforce of the Tatas was a lot freer than their counterparts anywhere else in India.

THE STEEL TOWN OF JAMSHEDPUR

It is inspiring to note that the approach that the Tatas adopted for labour welfare at Tata Steel was comprehensive in its scope, and not as patchwork benefits. The Group endeavoured to cater to all aspects of the workers' lives, including their civic needs, housing, health and education. In this context, the best example is the manner in which the Tata Group empowered the town of Jamshedpur.

Effectively, the town of Jamshedpur is maintained and managed to a large extent by Tata Steel. The company provides free municipal services to its employees. Even in the 1990s, which were loss-making years for the Tatas, the Group continued its annual expenses on the maintenance of Jamshedpur's civic amenities which were as high as ₹100 crore.[162]

The foundation for the steel town of Jamshedpur was laid back in 1917 when most of industrial England was highly underdeveloped. Sir Dorabji Tata consulted with two social scientists—Sidney and Beatrice Webb—as well as professors from London University to discuss the establishment of various services in Jamshedpur, such as social structures, medical facilities and cooperatives.

---

[162]Sudipt Dutta and Ranjna Kocherry, 'Learning to Survive', *Business India*, 13–26 July 1998, quoted in Shashank Shah, *The Tata Group: From Torchbearers to Trailblazers*, Penguin Random House India Private Limited, 2018, Kindle edition

The efforts of the Tata Group showed brilliant results in a very short period. In 1907, when the construction of the plant began, there was no urban settlement in Sakchi, a small village near the chosen site. But by 1951, Jamshedpur was a thriving township with a significant population of 2,18,000!

Here are the main areas in which Tata Steel concerted its efforts to build Jamshedpur:

1. HOUSING

During 1917 to 1950, the Tata Group built nearly 20,000 housing provisions (quarters, flats and bungalows) for its employees, and these were allotted based on seniority and salary in the company.[163] Thus a person in senior management or higher salary would be entitled to accommodation. For other workers who wanted to build their own homes, the Group also provided the required loans.

2. EDUCATION

The Tata Group focused on education, ensuring that the workers' children had access to schooling facilities. In the township, the Group built thirty-nine primary schools and five high schools. The medium of instruction varied; as many as eight languages were commonly used in these educational facilities. Besides running several schools for the employees'

---

[163] Shashank Shah, *The Tata Group: From Torchbearers to Trailblazers*, Penguin Random House India Private Limited, 2018. Kindle edition, Location 4923 of 8284

children in Jamshedpur, the company also reimbursed the tuition fees for the children studying elsewhere.

At the time the steel town was first built, the pan-India literacy rate was a measly 10 per cent. However, the literacy rate among Tata employees was 70 per cent![164]

3. MEDICAL FACILITIES

The Tatas built the Tata Main Hospital in Jamshedpur in 1908. It is currently a secondary care hospital with 914 beds and provides free healthcare services to all the employees and their families. The hospital extends free medical services even to the retired employees and the family members of deceased employees. The hospital has ample mobile medical vans to cater not only to Jamshedpur but also to the neighbouring villages.

The hospital has consistently played a significant role in uplifting the quality of life in the region. It has also helped mitigate the risks of epidemics. For instance, in 1974, the Chota Nagpur region in East India became the epicentre of the smallpox epidemic. To help contain the damage, the World Health Organization (WHO) requested the collaboration of Tata Steel. In response, Tata Steel sent in several medical resources and manpower, vaccinating people across 20,500 villages and eight-two towns in six months.[165] The efforts

---

[164]'The House of Tata', *Fortune*, 1 January 1944, quoted in Shashank Shah, *The Tata Group: From Torchbearers to Trailblazers*, Penguin Random House India Private Limited, 2018, Kindle edition, Location 4923 of 8284
[165]The Penguin India Blog, '15 Things You Didn't Know About "The Tata Group"', *The Penguin Digest*, 18 January 2019, https://penguin.co.in/thepenguindigest/15-things-you-didnt-know-about-the-tata-group/

initiated by Tata Steel helped eradicate smallpox from India. In 1975, India was declared free of smallpox—a historic achievement for a developing nation.

THE TAJ ATTACKS

The year 2008 came with a horrendous setback for the Tata Group. It was a year that shook the entire world. On 26 November 2008 (26/11), the Taj Hotel in Mumbai suffered a heinous terrorist attack that was shocking in its sheer intensity and impact. Several people lost their lives while many others had to be shifted to hospitals. In the aftermath of this heartbreaking incident, the Tata Group remained steadfast in its philosophy of touching lives through a positive social impact.

Many of the injured who had been shifted to various nearby hospitals had nobody to pay their hospital bills. These hospitals also had injured people from other affected sites, including from another hotel nearby, which also had been similarly attacked. Requests for help came in aplenty. It became difficult for the Tatas to ascertain if the requests were coming in from patients who had even been connected to the tragedy in their hotel in any manner. If not, should the Tata Group still pay the hospital bills for these patients?

Mr Ratan Tata made a simple decision to address the situation: make no discrimination. He sent Mr Krishna Kumar, a director of Tata Sons at that time, to the Taj with this message. The instruction stated that there should be no difference in the help extended to people, whether they were security personnel, police officers, fire servicemen, hotel employees, guests of the Taj or even the general public. The ambit even covered hawkers and street vendors injured during the attack. This applied irrespective of whether the victim had been injured at the Taj hotel or elsewhere in the city.

To pay for the hospital expenses of all the injured during the 26/11 attacks, the Tata Group decided to form a Trust. It was announced on 15 December 2008—only seventeen days after the disaster—and called the Taj Public Service Welfare Trust. It extended assistance not only to the victims of the Taj attacks but also to those affected by natural or man-made calamities in the years to come. This Trust received its funds from IHCL, Sir Dorabji Tata Trust and Sir Ratan Tata Trust; the latter two committed a significant initial contribution to get things started. Mr Ratan Tata was also on the Board of trustees along with Mr Krishna Kumar and Mr Raymond Bickson, the former Managing Director and CEO of IHCL, among others.

The Tata Group did everything in its power to heal those injured in the 26/11 attacks. Mr Ratan Tata instructed his team to visit every hospital where the injured were being treated. The team was responsible for ensuring that the bills had been taken care of. If the bills were pending, the Taj would do the needful.

The Tatas also went the extra mile to lend a helping hand to the families of the deceased. While nothing could make up for the loss of life, the Tatas announced several relief measures that would, at least, mitigate the financial woes that follow the death of the earning member of the household. The most significant of these was the decision to pay the families of the deceased Taj employees the corresponding salaries for the rest of their lives. The families would also be provided medical benefits and educational facilities (for dependents up to the age of 24 years).

What is worth noting here is that the Tatas did not delay the announcement of these measures or wait to analyse the repercussions in detail. They found these measures essential for healing and rolled them out within a week of the attack. The family members of all the deceased and injured employees were flown into Mumbai, where Mr Ratan Tata personally met them and shared the Group's decisions on the relief measures.

The Tata Group's reaction to the Taj attacks and the mature manner in which it dealt with the disaster reflects its humanitarian culture. The company's reaction aligned with its mission to contribute to the society, stepping up to help and heal when the situation so demanded it. Handling a tragedy of this magnitude isn't straightforward even for a business empire as huge as the Tata Group. But taking recourse in its long-held tradition of social welfare helped the Tatas mitigate the damage to some extent and earn tremendous goodwill in the process. (Though to clarify, earning the goodwill was never the objective but just a side effect.)

Perhaps the most surprising outcome of the tragedy was the swift turnaround time that the Tatas managed to achieve. Within three weeks of the attack, the Taj reopened its doors to guests. It was an action that inspired not only awe but also courage and an indomitable human spirit.

It is also laudable how the Tatas resumed the operations

of the Taj without undertaking any major retrenchment in its sizeable employee base of 1,800 people. After all, almost two-thirds of the hotel was still closed down, and it was natural to expect any organization to cut down on its employee base. But the Tatas opted to invest this time in employee training and improving the levels of service. Some employees were transferred to other Taj properties. Opting to retain the workforce even at the potential cost of incurring losses reflects the Tata's order of priorities: social well-being over profit, particularly in the wake of tragedy.

TAKEAWAY

In its illustrious history, the Tata Group has received several opportunities to create a positive social impact. It has grabbed these opportunities enthusiastically, sometimes at the cost of sacrificing greater profits in an alternate direction. It is this deep-rooted philosophy that the Group has followed that has given it the humane reputation it enjoys today.

The social impact that the Tata Group has created through its employee benefits reflects the enormity of the vision of its leaders. Mr Jamsetji Tata, for instance, considered the needs of his workers even long before the steel plant in Jamshedpur was established. He realized that a conducive work environment, shorter working hours and provisions such as provident fund and gratuity would ultimately contribute towards building an empowered and loyal workforce. He rolled out these benefits much before they were made statutory in workplaces around the globe. It is only logical that the planned city with

Choose Your Priorities Wisely: Positive Social Impact vs Profit 131

greenery and commendable civic amenities came to be called Jamshedpur.

Herein also lies a fine learning about effecting social change in the country of operation: choose to nurture instead of offering charity. The Tata Group has continuously invested in uplifting people from poverty and offering them opportunities to receive a world-class education that would equip them for the competitive job market. Mr Jamsetji Tata upheld that it was essential to nourish the brain, not dumb down the intellect by offering charity without a purpose. The establishment of the J.N. Tata Endowment Trust was a step to further this mission. The Trust has long helped Indian students to pursue higher studies overseas. In fact, at one time, two out of every five Indians joining the elite Indian Civil Services were Tata scholars.[166]

In the trying time of the Taj attacks, the Tatas showed no hesitation in rising to the occasion. Their philanthropy touched some of those who faced the brunt. Media reports suggest that the Taj employees went beyond their call of duty, even shielding the guests from attack. The Tata Group's decision to cover the medical expenses of all the victims across the city was a humanitarian act, way beyond any commercial considerations.

It is possible that such a strong intent in doing the right thing along with the determination of the Taj employees to bounce back helped the Taj reopen—within just three weeks of an event of such magnitude! This is an attitude that speaks of defiance and courage beyond measure—lessons that can equip

---

[166] Accessed in April 2019, http://www.tatasteel100.com/people/index.asp

business leaders and managers with the power of resilience and courage and grit to perform beyond expectations. In fact, in tragic circumstances it is the strength of the human spirit that shines, bringing out the best in some people. The Tatas showed this in spades when they, along with their people, stood alongside the others, in trying to heal wounds which affected a large number of the residents of Mumbai.

In 2010, Mr Barack Obama, the President of the USA at the time, commenced a historic ten-day visit to India. He chose the Taj as his residence in Mumbai as a gesture of solidarity with the victims of 26/11. During the visit, he paid an effective tribute to all those who been affected by the deplorable attack:

> There has been a great commentary on our decision to begin our visit here, in this dynamic city at this historic hotel. Those who have asked whether this is intended to send a message, my answer is simply, absolutely.[167]

---

[167] PTI, 'My stay is powerful message against terror: Obama', *The Economic Times*, 6 November 2010, accessed 14 May 2019, https://economictimes.indiatimes.com/news/politics-and-nation/my-stay-at-taj-is-powerful-message-against-terror-obama/articleshow/6879499.cms

14
ADOPT GLOBAL STANDARDS FROM THE OUTSET

BUILD AND GROW YOUR BUSINESS BY INTERNATIONAL STANDARDS, EVEN IF THE DOMESTIC INDUSTRY SEEMS TO ACCEPT LOWER STANDARDS.

For a business empire perceived to be as 'Indian' at heart as the Tata Group, it can be easy to fall into the comfort of complacency. Many businesses don't attempt to explore the global arena when they have their feet firmly entrenched in the domestic market where they enjoy significant success. However, as the experience of the Tatas has proved, adopting world-class standards from the very beginning is not only beneficial, but it is also an integral part of growth.

THE TAJ MAHAL HOTEL

The epitome of royalty that the Taj Mahal Hotel has become

has an incredible backstory. A famous anecdote goes that Mr Jamsetji Tata was once denied entry into a rather second-rate hotel. Some people believe that it was the Watson Hotel, where he had gone for lunch one afternoon.[168] Apparently, the hotel was reserved for 'Europeans only', and Mr Jamsetji Tata was, obviously, Indian.[169] The incident is said to have aggrieved him deeply. He decided to construct a luxurious hotel for Indians—an establishment that would be unparalleled in style and glory.

The above is, of course, an anecdote that has not been verified. Although there is no historical evidence found for the story, it is reasonable to assume that Mr Jamsetji Tata had a strong interest in making his business global from the very outset.

In building the Taj Hotel, Mr Jamsetji Tata did not calculate the costs upfront. No expense was spared for this project—a unique enterprise for the Tata Group until then. In fact, Mr Jamsetji Tata was so passionate about the project that much of the money spent in the construction of the hotel did not come from Tata Sons, but his personal funds (over ₹20 lakh).[170]

---

[168]Humanities 54: The Urban Imagination/Julie Buckler, Samuel Hazzard Cross Professor of Slavic and Comparative Literatures, Harvard University, accessed on 24 April 2019, http://hum54-15.omeka.fas.harvard.edu/exhibits/show/mumbai_development/taj; quoting Jatin Shah, 'History of Taj Mahal Palace Hotel & Tower, Mumbai', *The Creativity Engine*. N.p., 12 March 2014

[169]Ibid.

[170]Shyamal Majumdar, 'The Story of Taj', *Business Standard*, 21 January 2013, accessed 25 April 2019, https://www.business-standard.com/

In 1893, the Group bought reclaimed land near Apollo Bunder, Mumbai, and the construction started in 1900.[171] Mr Jamsetji Tata also planned to purchase two islands near Uran, a coastal town in the Raigad district, for the guests at the Taj to enjoy picnics.

The construction was a story in itself. The visionary leader travelled around the world to source the fittings, design elements and luxurious additions he felt were essential to make the hotel truly global. The electrical machinery came from Dusseldorf, Germany, while the chandeliers were sourced from Berlin, Germany. The Taj Hotel was the first building in Mumbai (then Bombay) to be lit up by electric lamps, the latest rage in lighting at the time. It is reported that the fans for the hotel rooms were bought from the USA. To keep the suites cool, the Tatas invested in a 15-tonne carbon dioxide ice-making plant. This mechanism was extremely new to India.

In terms of architecture too, the Taj Hotel was second to none. The steel pillars were based on a design that Mr Jamsetji Tata had seen in the Paris Exhibition (in 1887). The overall architecture of the hotel was an artistic combination of Moorish domes, Florentine Renaissance, and Oriental and Rajput styles.

Finally, on 16 December 1903, the Taj Hotel was inaugurated, presided by the now ailing industrialist. On the day of the inauguration, the first wing with two floors had been completed. The hotel welcomed seventeen guests on that first day.

---

article/beyond-business/the-story-of-taj-111121700080_1.html
[171]Ibid.

In building the Taj as a world-class hotel, Mr Jamsetji Tata had a clear mission: he wanted to attract people to visit India. He also wanted to prove that Indians could adopt global standards and come up with excellent results. Indeed, the Taj Mahal Hotel succeeded in fulfilling this goal. It laid the foundations for putting Mumbai on the global tourist map; many travel agents recommended that their clients include Mumbai in their itineraries so that they could stay at the Taj![172] Today, almost a century later, the Taj Hotel continues to be the preferred choice of royalty.[173]

THE GLOBAL ROOTS OF TATA STEEL

Mr Jamsetji Tata held on to three firm beliefs throughout his life. For India to develop, he felt, three projects were imperative:

- An iron and steel plant
- A hydroelectric power plant
- A world-class science educational institution to enrich the young minds in India

It is true that none of his dreams was fully realized during his lifetime. However, he had succeeded in ensuring that the seeds for these projects were definitely sown during his time. His successors, managed to bring all three of his dream projects to fruition.

---

[172] Shashank Shah, *The Tata Group: From Torchbearers to Trailblazers*, Penguin Random House India Private Limited, 2018. Kindle edition
[173] Ibid.

Adopt Global Standards from the Outset

It is perhaps the dream of setting up an iron and steel plant in India that Mr Jamsetji Tata held closest to his heart. He was of the firm belief that a nation could not achieve industrial greatness if it did not manufacture iron and steel. This belief was decidedly ahead of the times. It can be traced back to the 1880s when he attended a lecture by Mr Thomas Carlyle, a Scottish philosopher, in Manchester. He had been visiting Manchester to check out new machinery for the Tata's textile mill. But by the end of the trip, his interest in iron and steel was stirred. Later, Mr Jamsetji Tata wrote in his scrapbook something he had heard in Mr Carlyle's speech and never since forgotten: 'The nation which gains control of iron soon acquires the control of gold.'[174] Mr Jamsetji Tata grew increasingly eager to establish a steel plant that could hold its own against the world's finest and most productive manufacturing units.

The actual fructification of this rousing dream, however, was an uphill task. The Indian political scenario at the time was not supportive of Indian industrialization. In fact, the British had not even allowed any private companies to operate in the mining sector. Moreover, India had missed the benefits of the industrial revolution—unlike many nations of the West. Under these circumstances, any industrial attempts seemed ambitious and maybe scary. In fact, at that time, the idea for a steel plant seemed so far-fetched that Sir Frederick Upcott, the then Chief Commissioner of the Great Indian Peninsular Railway, expressed his sarcasm:

---

[174]Tata Steel Centenary website, accessed 25 April 2019, http://www.tatasteel100.com/people/feel-for-steel.asp

> Do you mean to say that the Tatas propose to make steel rails to British specifications? Why, I will undertake to eat every pound of steel rail they [the Tatas] succeed in making.[175]

Another anecdote mentions that it was a good thing that Mr Upcott had not been alive when the first ingot rolled out from the Tata Steel plant a few years later, else he would have had a real stomach pain!

Mr Jamsetji Tata remained undaunted. Driven by his mission which led him to possess the perseverance and dedication to tackle the adversities that came before him. He patiently waited for the right opportunity. In 1899, his opportunity arrived. The demand for steel overtook its supply, thanks largely to the defence and railroad sectors, and Lord Curzon, the Viceroy of British India during the period, was forced by his superiors to liberalize the mining laws. Mr Jamsetji Tata grabbed this opportunity. He travelled to England to meet Lord Hamilton in 1900, the Secretary of State for India and the only person who could issue orders to the viceroy to grant the Tatas the permission to set up the steel mills.

In the run-up to the establishment of the steel plant, Mr Jamsetji Tata conducted massive research and groundwork. He travelled across America to gather the expertise and understand the best technologies for the plant. For instance, he studied the coking processes at Birmingham and Alabama and visited the ore markets in Cleveland. Finally, he decided

---

[175] Tata Steel Centenary website, accessed 25 April 2019, http://www.tatasteel100.com/people/index.asp

to rope in the services of Kennedy, Sahlin & Co. for the proposed steel plant. Kennedy, Sahlin & Co. was the best firm in metallurgical engineering. The arrangement was finalized at Pittsburgh, where Mr Jamsetji Tata met Mr Julian Kennedy, one of the partners of the firm.

Although Mr Jamsetji Tata had invested so much energy in researching the finest for his dream plant, it still remained a risky venture. During the meeting at Pittsburgh, Mr Kennedy apprised him of some of the main risks: long investigative procedures and immense expenditure. But having come so far, and infused with such zeal about the project, Mr Jamsetji Tata refused to be held back. Mr Kennedy directed him to Mr Charles Page Perin, a reputed surveyor. Years later, Mr Perin recounted his first meeting with the Tata founder:[176]

> I was poring over some accounts in the office when the door opened and a stranger in a strange garb entered. He walked in, leaned over my desk and looked at me fully a minute in silence.
>
> Finally, he said in a deep voice, 'Are you Charles Page Perin?'
>
> I said, 'Yes'.
>
> He stared at me again silently for a long time, and then slowly he said, 'I believe I have found the man I have been looking for. Julian Kennedy has written (to) you that I am going to build a steel plant in India. I want you to come to India with me, to find suitable iron ore

---

[176]Tata Steel Centenary website, accessed 25 April 2019, http://www.tatasteel100.com/heritage/history/history01.asp

and coking coal and the necessary fluxes. I want you to take charges as my consulting engineer. Mr. Kennedy will build the steel plant wherever you advise and I will foot the bill. Will you come to India with me?'

I was dumbfounded, naturally. But you don't know what character and force radiated from Tata's face. And kindliness, too. 'Well', I said, 'Yes, I'd go.' And I did.

In 1912, the first ingots rolled out from the steel production plant. By 2001, Tata Steel became one of the lowest-cost producers of steel in the world. As of 2019, it is one of the leading steel companies in the world.

THE INDIAN INSTITUTE OF SCIENCE (IISC)

We already examined how Mr Jamsetji Tata wanted to set up a university of science in India that would work to train young minds and infuse students with a scientific temperament. In 1898, he created an endowment for establishing such an institution. Interestingly, the foundation for this institution also has an incredible backstory, along the lines of the inception of the Taj Hotel.

The anecdote goes that Mr Jamsetji Tata once happened to meet Swami Vivekananda, the renowned monk and disciple of Ramakrishna, on a ship. The two men discussed Mr Jamsetji Tata's ongoing research for the steel project. Apparently, the Tata founder was carrying sacks of earth from different regions of India to test for iron ore deposits in Germany. Swami Vivekananda offered a better suggestion: why not set up an institution that could do this in India instead?

Adopt Global Standards from the Outset

However, much like the steel project, this dream was also embroiled in adversity. The Tatas failed to receive the required permissions from Lord Curzon, the incumbent Viceroy of British India.

Mr Jamsetji Tata refused to give up. He promptly pledged almost half his fortune (which consisted of fourteen buildings and four other properties at the time and was worth ₹30 lakh) towards the institute. The sum would be equivalent to almost ₹100 crore in 2018. This was an unprecedented gesture which drew appreciation from everyone around Jamsetji. But the British still did not budge from their stand. They continued to refuse permission and expected that the funds would be diverted to the Tata's industrial projects instead. Consequently, the money remained untouched for a long while. Mr Jamsetji Tata had left clear instructions for his sons in his will: the funds set aside for the institute must only be used for the purpose they had been allotted.

Finally, a year after the death of Mr Jamsetji Tata, Lord Curzon granted permission. The land for the institute (370 acres) came in as a donation from Krishna Raja Wadiyar IV, the Maharaja of Mysore. In 1911, IISc opened its doors to students.

IISc has proved to be a wonderful example of global standards in action. It has consistently ranked amongst the best universities in India and amongst the top fifty globally. It has produced Nobel laureates, trained many of India's greatest scientists, and nurtured some of India's finest scientific institutions.[177]

---

[177] Tata Website, accessed 25 April 2019, https://www.tata.com/

One could even refer to the micromanagement and attention that Mr J.R.D. Tata gave to the then nascent Air India, which made it into an airline that the others looked up to, and tried to emulate. The Singapore government wanting to tie up with the Tatas to set up their new airline, at the time, also speaks volumes of the high standards that the Tatas had imbibed in Air India at the time.

TAKEAWAY

There is one vital lesson that emerges from the multiple instances when the Tatas have embraced global standards. In the modern world, business leaders must not be complacent. While the present situation within a company might be lucrative and promising, the tide can turn unexpectedly. When it does, only an organization that has adopted world-class practices can hope to remain afloat.

In adopting international standards for business, it is also important to keep an eye focused on one's dreams. Believing in the power of dreams, backed by the will to carry it out, will help guide the organization towards success.

Mr Jamsetji Tata, the man behind the vision of the Taj Hotel, Tata Steel and IISc, could not see his dreams come true during his lifetime. However, they eventually came to life—and have performed gloriously since then—only because he firmly believed that they would. The grandeur of the Taj Hotel, for example, is equivalent to any leading hotel in Europe; its elegance makes it rank year after year among the best hotels in

---

community/education/indian-institute-of-science

the world. Likewise, both Tata Steel and IISc have consistently delivered on their promise of furthering India's economic and social development. Similarly, Mr J.R.D. Tata's Air India having high standards, which won it international recognition and fame, speaks volumes of the high standards that existed then. This pleasant reality of today has its foundation in several years ago, when the Tatas decided to keep their eyes on the global arena and for the future, despite the then prevailing environments discouraging them from doing so.

Another factor worth noting is the patience and determination the Tata chairmen had, in pursuit of their dreams. They faced numerous adversities and were not given permissions, but they waited patiently, and then grabbed the opportunities when they came.

15
TO EXPERIENCE SUCCESS, FIRST ENVISION IT CLEARLY

DEVELOP A CLEAR VISION FOR YOUR BUSINESS AND ALIGN YOUR STRATEGIES AND OPERATIONS WITH IT.

An integral factor in the Tata Group's success has been the vision of its leaders. Through the years, the chairmen of the Group have demonstrated tremendous clarity of vision and led the business empire forward in a manner which is aligned with it. It would be a mistake to assume a 'visionary' approach to be an obsolete thought, important only for legacy companies but relevant for today's practical, grounded world. Having a distinct vision for your business will always be critical, and, without it, the best-laid plans for growth can become chaotic.

JAMSETJI TATA'S VISION: THE COURAGE TO DREAM

The proclivity of the Tata Group towards developing a vision started right from its founder, Mr Jamsetji Tata. He was committed to the economic progress of India and dreamed of three projects to further this goal. As we discussed in Chapter 14, Mr Jamsetji Tata envisioned a hydroelectric power plant, a steel plant and a world-class scientific educational institution. He even gave up half his wealth to accumulate the corpus needed for building the educational institution, which, subsequently, became IISc. Today, IISc is acknowledged as one of the top fifty universities in the world.

Mr Jamsetji Tata's vision was ambitious and far reaching; some might call it grandiose. He dreamed of establishing a hydroelectric plant in India back in 1875—a time when even the US, arguably much more industrially developed than India at the time, did not have one. In fact, the first commercial-scale hydroelectric project was built in Wisconsin, USA, only in 1882. This was seven years after Mr Jamsetji Tata had proposed this concept for India!

Eventually, his vision did come true, albeit posthumously. While his proposals for setting up power plants on the Narmada river and in Goa had been refused earlier, the project saw the light of day in 1915. Sir Dorabji Tata, his son, was successful in setting up a power plant on the foothills of the Western Ghats in Khopoli, near Mumbai, Maharashtra.

The hydroelectric power project was a complicated venture to realize not only because of political and economic limitations but also because of its sheer scale. As Mr Jamsetji Tata had envisioned it, the project would require over 7,000 workers.

It would also need pipelines from Germany, waterwheels from Switzerland, generators from America, and cables from England—all this on the steep slopes of Lonavala and Khandala in the Western Ghats near Mumbai. But in bringing this project to completion, the Tata Group ensured that the reality was in line with the grand vision. One of the three dams that were constructed was larger than even the Aswan Dam on the River Nile in Egypt! This is even more commendable considering that the project was launched just fourteen years after the Niagara Falls hydropower project in 1882.

After the plant was inaugurated in February 1915, even the British government was forced to compliment the Tatas on their achievements, commenting that it symbolized the confidence that Indians had in their abilities. The project was significant for the time, as the power station at Khopoli, Maharashtra was the largest in India while the pipes feeding water to the station were the longest in the world![178]

Mr Jamsetji Tata's vision is also evident in his pursuit of the Taj Mahal Hotel project in Mumbai (see Chapter 14). It was, in the truest sense, more a labour of love than a commercial venture. He personally handpicked all the equipment, furnishings and fittings for the hotel from all over the world, aiming to create a property that could be compared to the world's most elegant. Back then, this was a vision that is certain to have come across as lofty. But this did not stop the Tata's visionary leader from keeping his chin up and believing in his dreams.

---

[178]Shashank Shah, *The Tata Group: From Torchbearers to Trailblazers*, Penguin Random House India Private Limited, 2018, Kindle edition

CARRYING ON A LEGACY: FROM MR JAMSETJI TATA TO MR N. CHANDRASEKARAN

As the Group chairman after Mr Jamsetji Tata, Sir Dorabji Tata also displayed the clarity of thought that had been so alluring about his father. He carried on the legacy, infusing it with his own perspective, and ensured that both Tata Steel and IISc finally saw the light of day. He propelled a fast-growing group into even more promising waters and carried on nation-building activities in his own way.

Sir Dorabji Tata was succeeded by Mr J.R.D. Tata, who displayed original thought along with a commendable understanding of the business landscape. His ability to dream big perhaps stemmed from his passion for aviation, where literally the sky was the limit. He is credited with steering the first-ever flight in India, back in 1932 from Karachi to Mumbai.

Along with an ambitious vision, Mr J.R.D. Tata also possessed great foresight. He was quick to identify the potential of the IT sector. In 1968, he set up TCS with a twelve-member staff. The firm would provide technical support and management consulting services to the subsidiaries of the Tata Group. From those humble origins, TCS has since grown to become one of the most profitable companies in the Tata Group today, and amongst the top three largest IT services companies in the world.[179] Mr J.R.D. Tata also set up

---

[179] Varun Sood, 'TCS set to become world's third-largest IT services company', LiveMint, 8 May 2019, accessed 14 May 2019, https://www.livemint.com/industry/infotech/tcs-set-to-become-world-s-third-largest-it-services-company-1557255142387.html

Tata Administrative Services (TAS) to ensure that the Group always had competent managers for the growing Tata empire. It was his long-term vision that helped consolidate the Group even when it ventured in newer directions, thereby paving the path for business progress alongside nation-building.

The exemplary vision of the Tata leaders continued unfazed with Mr Ratan Tata—a chairman under whom the Group was able to consolidate itself into a cohesive empire. He extended the Tata ownership over its various companies and modernized the eighty-odd companies so that they could compete in a changing world. Aware of the transforming domestic market, he also led the Group to tap foreign markets. Under his leadership, the Tata Group managed to bring in a substantial part of its group revenue from international businesses and clients.

We examined the story of the Indica back in Chapter 4. When Mr Ratan Tata pushed Tata Motors to develop India's first indigenous passenger vehicle, it was the foundation for an even bigger dream. The idea was to make cars affordable for the larger audience. Mr Ratan Tata possessed a deep sense of social responsibility and the desire to contribute to the upliftment of society. This could be done by creating more jobs and improving access to goods and services— even ones like motor cars that had always been deemed as luxuries. (This subsequently led to the development of Tata Nano—a car that was available for only ₹1 lakh ($2,500). The Nano was designed in a modular manner so that it could be sold in kits that could then be distributed, assembled and serviced by local entrepreneurs. We will study the Nano in more detail in see Chapter 16.). The lack of commercial success notwithstanding, the Tatas had the courage to dream big and to execute flawlessly in pursuit of the vision, to help the mid to lower segments of the society have access to low-cost cars.

Mr Ratan Tata was succeeded by Mr Cyrus Mistry who sought to bring more accountability and profitability within the Group. In his short tenure, he worked extensively on consolidating the Group and critically examining all the individual companies for profitability and strategic fit.

The current chairman, Mr Natarajan Chandrasekaran, is the first non-Parsi and non-family chairman of the Group. He has been at the helm since 2017. It is still too early for a judgement to be made about his larger vision for the empire, so I shall refrain from doing so. But he is carrying on the work of consolidation, and addressing the long pending issues which had become increasingly important.

TAKEAWAY

The ability to dream big and display the commitment to see these dreams through is a common thread tying the chairpersons of the Tata Group until date. From the very outset, the Group has enjoyed the personal attention of people who have been not only empire builders but also visionary entrepreneurs. This has been a gift that has helped the Group achieve much of the success it has achieved till today.

Not every business leader may be blessed with a vision. The power to dream does not come easily or to everyone.

What, perhaps, made it easier for the Tatas was that each of their visions was founded on their core philosophy: the pursuit of nation-building. Envisioning a concept that helped further economic and social progress and then seeing it through with integrity and patience has been the underlying theme determining the Tata Group's actions. This is a theme that runs contrary to the popular concept of a 'capitalist' or even 'industrialist'; the term has come to be associated with someone who is interested in pursuing profits at any cost. The Tatas have chosen deliberately and consciously, to walk down this path. Their companies have reported reduced profits, as they chose to work on philanthropy and social welfare, instead of the pursuit of sheer profits. And this is a trade-off they are willing to make. The Tatas, choose to remain true to their vision, even if it means behaving contrary to this commonly held perception of an industrialist. In their heart of hearts, they remain what they have always been, nation builders.

In 1965, a Kolkata-based schoolteacher asked Mr J.R.D. Tata to reflect on the principles that guided him during his lifetime. What he shared summarises the lessons from this chapter excellently:[180]

> I do not consider myself to be an 'illustrious personality' but only an ordinary businessman and citizen who has tried to make the best of his opportunities to advance the

---

[180] Letter from J.R.D. Tata Tata letter to K.C. Bhansali, 13 September 1965, cited in Arvind Mambro, editor, Letters: J.R.D. Tata, (Rupa & Co. New Dehli:, 2004), p. 87-88,

cause of India's industrial and economic development. Any such guiding principles I might unconsciously have had in my life can be summarised as follows:

- That nothing worthwhile is ever achieved without deep thought and hard work;
- That one must think for oneself and never accept at face value slogans and catchphrases to which, unfortunately, our people are too easily susceptible;
- That one must forever strive for excellence or even perfection, in any task however small and never be satisfied with second best;
- That no success or achievement in material terms is worthwhile unless it serves the needs or interests of the country and its people and is achieved by fair and honest means;
- That good human relations not only bring great personal rewards but are essential to the success of any enterprise.

Now, that demonstrates a unique mix of the ideal and the practical, the visionary and the real. One is left wondering... What heights could the Group have achieved had it been unshackled from the start, allowed to execute its planned projects without any restrictions? I guess we will never know.

16

THE TATA NANO: MEGA LESSONS FROM THE SMALL CAR

FOLLOW A DREAM WITH A SOCIAL SIDE.

The Tata Nano's is a fascinating tale with several important lessons for business leaders and managers.

> *It... [The thought behind the Nano] is propelled by the opportunity, but there is also a social or dreamy side to it... Today in India, you often see four people on a scooter... It's a dangerous form of transportation... If we can make something available on four wheels—all-weather and safe—then I think we will have done something for that mass of young Indians.... I believe there would be a market potential of 1 million cars a year.*   —Mr Ratan Tata[181]

---

[181] *McKinsey Quarterly*, 'What's next for the Tata Group?' 31 October

The story of the Tata Nano is one of the most riveting chapters in the history of the Tata Group. It is also an episode replete with vital lessons for both group insiders and business leaders who wish to launch original ventures founded on a clear thought.

As Mr Ratan Tata's statement reveals, the genesis for the Nano was in his observation of a typical Indian family on a scooter. He felt a pressing need to do something for this vast segment of the population for whom a scooter was clearly inadequate but also the only affordable option. What if the Tatas could develop a car that would be affordable for them?

During a media interview, Mr Ratan Tata was questioned about the estimated cost of such a vehicle. He pitched it between the cost of a two-wheeler and a cheap four-wheeler—somewhere in the vicinity of ₹1 lakh. This tempting price point received widespread media coverage. Since it had got stuck in the minds of the media and potential customers alike, Mr Ratan Tata challenged his team to adhere to this price point. The Tatas would endeavour to come up with a car within the price that the media had popularized.

The Tata Group started on developing the Nano with full gusto. Mr Ratan Tata instructed his team of engineers to build a low-cost car that would revolutionize personal transport in India. Finally, in March 2009, the Nano was launched. It cost only ₹1 lakh. Mr Ratan Tata had kept his promise.

However, the project faced several difficulties before the first car could roll out from the assembly lines. Before the Nano could start large-scale manufacturing, their plant in Singur,

---

2005, accessed in April 2019, https://www.forbes.com/2005/10/28/india-software-tata-cx_1028mckinsey.html#2d5114cd235a

West Bengal faced major issues related to land acquisition. The opposition party in West Bengal at the time was against the project, claiming that the plant would displace thousands of farmers. The party also complained that the land had been acquired under dubious circumstances and demanded that 400 acres of the acquired property be returned to the farmers.[182] Things became ugly and violence broke out, hence the Tatas were compelled to relocate the plant. In September 2008, work at the Singur plant was suspended.

The Nano plant was then moved to Sanand, Gujarat—geographically on the other side of India and 1,500 kilometres away from the earlier location. Understandably, this was a monumental expense. Mr Ratan Tata offered to bear 75 per cent of the relocation costs that the forty-six primary vendors, who had followed the Tatas to Singur, would have to incur to shift to Sanand.

In January 2010, the shifting was finally complete, and trial production began in the Sanand factory. However, the costs incurred in the whole process were certain to weigh things down. The Nano also suffered the brunt of the 2008 global meltdown. The financial crisis adversely affected the auto sector and the Nano, too, was a victim.

At the time of its launch, the Nano received rave reviews. It also received 203,000 fully paid orders by May 2009.[183] It was

---

[182] Palepu, Krishna G., Bharat N. Anand and Rachna Tahilyani. 'Tata Nano–The People's Car'. Harvard Business School Case 710-420, April 2010. (Revised March 2011.)

[183] Sebastian Blanco, 'Tata receives 203,000 bookings for Nano, twice what they can initially fulfil', Autoblog.com, 5 May 2009, accessed 14 May 2019, https://www.autoblog.com/2009/05/05/tata-receives-203-000-bookings-

expected that once the first batch of cars hit the markets, the volumes would shoot up further, riding on positive customer feedback. Unfortunately, this never happened.

WHY DIDN'T THE NANO TAKE OFF?

The Nano was expected to usher in a new era: the age of catering to ultra-low-cost consumers. Mr Ratan Tata was compared to Henry Ford, the automobile pioneer, for opening up a new segment of customers, who would be able to buy a car, something which they probably thought would have been out of their reach till then. This was akin to what Henry Ford had done a century ago, ushering in mass-produced automobiles. But despite the Tata's best intentions, the product did not achieve the success that they expected it to be.

The reasons behind the failure seemed to pertain to the product itself. There were media reports of the car allegedly catching fire, which created safety concerns and triggered negative publicity around the vehicle.[184] Although the Tatas did their best to resolve these issues, the damage to the reputation was done. But more importantly, the failure can be attributed to misplaced perceptions. The Nano was 'cheap'— not something that announced aspiration or ambition for the class of consumers that the Tata Group was targeting. Yes, these were two-wheeler owners who wished to upgrade to a

---

for-nano-twice-what-they-can-ini/
[184]Ashish Kumar Mishra, 'Tata's Nano: Fire!' 21 May 2010, accessed 27 May 2019, https://www.forbes.com/2010/05/20/forbes-india-wheels-of-fire-tata-moters.html#68053b147bd6

four-wheeler, but not when the option was perceived as cheap.

The Tatas initiated several measures to encourage a pick-up in the sales. In 2015, they offered superior features such as a hatchback and an automatic transmission. But none of these measures seems to have worked. In 2019, the company sold a mere 376 cars—a far cry from 2011–12 when it sold 74,527 units.[185]

It is expected that the company would announce the closure of its Nano plant. The project is rumoured to be very close to Mr Ratan Tata, and this can explain why it is still operational amidst such severe setbacks. Some press reports in 2019 even highlighted glaring losses of ₹1,000 crore—something that Mr Cyrus Mistry, the former chairman, had also pointed out.[186]

TAKEAWAY

Although the market may have written off the Tata Nano as a gigantic loss, it does provide invaluable business lessons.

First, the Tata Nano is the perfect example of the importance of understanding one's consumers and their psyche. Even the best products made with the right intentions may fail if they are unable to understand the thought process of the target audience. The Tata's purpose was noble—to help out a class of consumers seeking to upgrade their lives.

---

[185]Sumant Banerji, 'Is it finally the end of Nano?' *Business Today*, 15 April 2019, accessed 27 April 2019, https://www.businesstoday.in/sectors/auto/is-it-finally-the-end-of-the-nano/story/337462.html
[186]Ibid.

The Tata Nano: Mega Lessons from the Small Car

The late Prof. C.K. Prahalad, a globally renowned business thinker, had stated that immense riches exist in serving the needs of the consumers at the bottom of the pyramid. Mr Ratan Tata wished to fulfil the needs and dreams of those consumers whom no one was addressing. This seems like a very profitable opportunity and a significant growth area which many companies are exploring, and at the first glance, seems very attractive.

However, the Tatas apparently lacked in their understanding of how this audience felt about purchasing a car. They saw a car as an aspirational symbol, a sign of social status. The Nano, on the other hand, came with the label of the 'cheapest car in the world'. It did not find favour with the customers because it screamed cheap, violating the very purpose and associated benefits of owning a car. Even so, the fact that the Tata Group employed massive resources in building a product for undervalued consumers speaks volumes of the Group's focus on a social cause. Although the final product was not a success, this sentiment deserves to be admired.

In 2013, I happened to visit the Sanand factory of Tata Nano with thirty students as a part of a student factory visit. The factory was shut for maintenance, and we were waiting in the reception area for the manager to escort us inside. We saw him arrive in a bright-yellow convertible—yes, a Nano. All of us were instantly drawn to the car. The manager told us it was only a pet project—a joke by some engineers built using a spare Nano. This 'pet project' cost only ₹1,50,000.

The students went ballistic. I distinctly remember how all thirty of them took out their credit cards, eager to pay an advance for the car! One enterprising budding student even collected cash by borrowing from his classmates, and offered to pay cash down. He was interested in buying the car on the spot! And, if that wasn't possible, could they please place advance orders? Soon, the 'experimental' Nano had about sixty-five orders. Ultimately though, we could not buy the car. The manager refused any such deals, in spite of some of the students offering to pay a 30 per cent premium if allowed to drive away with the vehicle there and then.

The incident made me wonder: could an altered positioning of the Nano have changed its fortunes? Would the final product have then received the kind of instant success that its souped-up version apparently did at the factory site that day? After all, had I just witnessed the Nano becoming repositioned from a poor man's car to another segment's 'toy'?

Another critical learning from the Nano story is the need to conduct extensive product testing before release. The Nano was already a highly watched launch, especially after all the media ire over its factory relocation problems. It was also a highly innovative and hitherto unexplored project idea. The team was under tremendous pressure to deliver. Under such circumstances, when there is so much riding on one project, pretesting might have been helpful. It could have alerted the team to some of the problems that went unnoticed and later blew up into a PR crisis for the Group, which could have contributed to the downfall.

The Nano and the reasons for its failure have been discussed extensively across the media and academia. A 2011 article in the *Harvard Business Review*[187] states that one needs to have flexibility to ensure project success. Pre-launch expectations need to be kept to a minimum to allow one to perfect post-launch corrections in the business model. Additionally, it is important to conceive a product that people will *want*—something that fulfils an unmet need, can be obtained at an attractive price point, and has a value proposition that is both well communicated and different from the competition. It makes sense for a company to proceed with a product only when it fulfils this basic criterion.

In all fairness, I must quite humbly point out to the readers that it is easy for me to comment from the stance of an armchair consultant, far removed from the pressures or even knowledge of the real-time environment. I appreciate that the circumstances for the Tata Group must have been quite stressful, and possibly I have definitely overlooked a lot of factors, which the experienced management at the Tata Motors would have had greater expertise in dealing with. But it is precisely situations like these that offer great learning opportunities. Learning from the past experiences of the Nano team can help managers increase their chances of success for new products. It is only with that intention, that I have discussed the above case in this chapter. In such cases, one must realize, it is more difficult to say with a high degree of surety what could have gone right, but easier to analyse what went wrong!

---

[187] Matt Eyring, 'Learning from Tata's Nano Mistakes', *Harvard Business Review* online, 11 January 2011, accessed 27 April 2019, https://hbr.org/2011/01/learning-from-tatas-nano-mista

17

EXITING IS NOT FAILURE

YOU MAY HAVE NOT PLANNED YOUR EXIT WELL IN ADVANCE, BUT WHEN A BUSINESS DOES NOT MAKE SENSE, DON'T HESITATE IN EXITING.

Historically, the Tatas have often been pulled up in the media for not exiting projects or companies that are loss-making. However, contrary to popular opinion, the Tata Group *has* exited ventures that it hasn't found profitable or aligned with the overall growth strategy. It has also periodically divested assets to reduce the losses from non-performing businesses. So, while the Tata Group has the workers' welfare in mind, it hasn't stopped them from making exits where necessary. It is important for managers and business leaders to understand the fine line between being persistent and unreasonably stubborn. Let us take a few examples to understand this.

By 2014, it became apparent that the Tata-DoCoMo deal was not working in the Group's favour. In an interview with

The Week, Mr N. Chandrasekaran, the incumbent Chairman of Tata Sons, admitted that Tata Teleservices was losing money every month.[188] It was getting difficult to revive the company. The company had a high debt of ₹34,000 crore, spectrum liabilities of ₹9,000 crore and payments due to DoCoMo of ₹9,000 crore. The total was ₹52,000 crore. The Tata Group could have invested more capital to the extent of about $10 million in the company, but the future would remain uncertain. In light of this apprehension, the Tatas decided to exit from this venture. They cleared the outstanding payment to DoCoMo and then sold the consumer division of Tata Teleservices to Bharti Airtel.

Another venture where the Tatas struggled with high debt was Tata Steel UK. The company was losing money, and the cost of servicing the debt was high. To contain the losses, the Tatas worked out a joint venture deal with ThyssenKrupp, merging their plants. It made financial sense and was also a good option for the Tatas to tackle the rising debt. However, the European Commission blocked the deal in May 2019, and both the companies were forced to abandon this plan.[189]

Back in 2005, Tata Steel had acquired NatSteel and Millennium Steel (Tata Steel Thailand) and managed to turn

---

[188]Riyad Mathew and Rachna Tyagi, 'N. Chandrasekaran: I want to simplify Tata Group', *The Week*, 14 October 2018, accessed 27 April 2019, https://www.theweek.in/theweek/cover/2018/10/05/n-chandrasekhar-i-want-to-simplify-tata-group.html

[189]Rakhi Mazumdar, 'Tata Steel, Tyseenkrupp set to abandon JV plans in Europe', *The Economic Times*, 11 May 2019, accessed 14 May 2019, https://economictimes.indiatimes.com/industry/indl-goods/svs/steel/tata-steel-thyssenkrupp-set-to-abandon-jv-plans-in-europe/articleshow/69268675.cms

them into profitable companies (see Chapter 8). However, eventually, the Group found it more profitable to do a stake sale. On 21 April 2019, the Tatas sold 70 per cent of their holdings in NatSteel and Tata Steel (Thailand) to the HBIS Group, a Chinese iron and steel manufacturer, for $327 million.[190]

Another interesting approach that the Tatas have explored in this regard is through mergers. In April 1993, the Group sold TOMCO to HLL. The merger was extensively covered by the local media; it was one of the most prominent deals in Indian corporate history. The merger gave HLL access to multiple brands in toilet soaps and hair oils, thus boosting the HLL portfolio.[191] Subsequently, in 1995, HLL and Lakme Ltd formed a joint venture (50:50) called Lakme Lever Ltd. This entity aimed to market Lakme's cosmetics, which was an undisputed leader in the Indian market. In 1998, Lakme sold its brands to HLL, along with divesting its 50 per cent stake in the joint venture, thus exiting from a non-core business.[192]

TAKEAWAY

It would be presumptuous for any businessperson to assume that all their ventures would witness success. The rational approach is to identify when an enterprise needs to be divested

---

[190] Keshav Sunkara, 'Tata Steel to sell majority stake in southeast Asia biz to China's HBIS', VCCCircle, 28 January 2019, accessed 27April 2019, https://www.vccircle.com/tata-steel-to-sell-majority-stake-in-southeast-asia-biz-to-china-s-hbis/;
[191] https://www.hul.co.in/about/who-we-are/our-history/
[192] Ibid.

from the current portfolio and then follow through on the exit without hesitation.

The Tata Group, as we just studied, has exited multiple businesses. Some of these exits have been led by financial reasons; the ventures which they exited from did not make economic sense for the Group. Some other divestments have intended to make the Group more focused and use the invested capital more judiciously. The final goal was to derive greater profits for the business. If this demanded that a company be divested to another, it needed to be done.

For the Tata Group, ensuring constant dividends was essential even more so because of its Trust-based structure. As Mr J.R.D. Tata once said, the Group needed to make profits, as its major shareholders were the Trusts.[193] And, if the dividends from the Tata Group were lowered, the Trusts could not work.

---

[193]Shashank Shah, *The Tata Group: From Torchbearers to Trailblazers*, Penguin Random House India Private Limited, 2018, Kindle edition

18
SUMMING UP: MANAGEMENT LESSONS FOR YOUR BUSINESS

The Tata Group has risen to the position of a business empire that the entire country looks up to. Not only is it a strong and profitable enterprise but also a name that inspires trust and goodwill in the society. This reputation is one that the Group has earned with considerable effort, supported by the vision and dedication of the leaders who have been at the helm at various times in its history. From Mr Jamsetji Tata to Mr Ratan Tata, as well as the present generation of highly trained professionals, the Tata Group has benefitted from competent managers with the desire to excel.

Let us recapitulate the management lessons we learnt from the Tata Group.

1. **Build your business with a long-term perspective, instead of focusing only on short-term gains**
   The Tata Group has initiated several projects that would

Summing Up: Management Lessons For Your Business   165

reap dividends only over time. These are choices that many contemporaries would have hesitated from making, primarily due to the absence (or paucity) of results in the immediate future. But projects like these have helped the Group emerge stronger with each passing year. The Tata Group's acquisition of JLR and subsequent decision to invest in new product research are good examples of this approach. The workers' benefits that Tata Steel rolled out in Jamshedpur, along with the setting up of schools and hospitals, are also testimony to the Tata's long-term perspective towards business.

2. **Don't compromise on your values and business ethics to achieve elusive growth. Frequently, doing the 'right' thing in business reaps more than just moral rewards**

    As a business grows, it becomes easier and more tempting to compromise on values and ethics that have held it in good stead so far. Taking a few unethical decisions might not seem like a big deal when the rewards are alluring enough. However, this can be a major pitfall, as compromises like these have a way of haunting a business empire for years to come.

    The Tata Group preferred to obtain a satisfactory answer to the 'is it right?' question for every major step, whether it pertained to tax avoidance or deciding whether or not to shut down Tata Steel in the face of complexities. It also chose not to close down companies if it felt wrong to do so, such as TOMCO, which had a three-year lock-in for HLL after the sale.

3. **Focus on building trust in your stakeholder universe, including partners, suppliers, employees as well as customers**

   Trust is one of the biggest blessings for a business, and it emanates from the people holding the reins. The Tata Group has consistently taken steps to keep its trust quotient intact; in fact, it has only grown stronger with time. The payments that the Group issued to KraussMaffei and Tata DoCoMo, possibly at great personal costs, reflects the Group's commitment to maintaining the trust it inspires. This reputation gives the Tatas a distinct edge in new business deals and partnerships.

4. **Depending on the scale and size of your business, invest in nation-building. Even if you find large-scale projects to be beyond your scope, building with a service mindset can reap rich dividends**

   Its contribution to nation-building is perhaps one of Tata's biggest accomplishments. The establishment of Tata Steel gave a major impetus to the domestic industrial landscape. Through Tata Motors, the Group pioneered the Indica and created a platform to exhibit indigenous design skills. The Group has also looked towards the defence sector, at a time when few peers are willing to bear the high costs and involved risks. Partnering in nation-building has helped the Group receive accolades that are both financial and moral.

5. **Do not curtail your dreams or attempt to make them less 'grand'. Dreams decide the vision of your business, and when executed with passion, can come true**

Business leaders should ideally also be dreamers. It is through the dreams we see for our business that we feel empowered to make great strides. The Tata Group dreamt of a steel plant, a power plant and an international-level educational institution at a time when much of India was highly underdeveloped. These dreams must have seemed impossible at the time. But all of them came true eventually.

6. **Develop a culture of nourishing visionaries in your business and grant them the freedom to operate with independence**

   The Tata Group has benefitted from various visionary leaders who have helped it scale new heights. It was Mr J.R.D. Tata's passion for aviation and the vision to pioneer quality air travel in India that led to the formation of Air India. The origins of the Taj Hotel, TCS and Tata Steel also lie in a clear, if ambitious, vision. Business leaders should strive to nurture such visionary individuals and teams in their companies and allow them the liberty of free thought.

7. **Exit from avenues that have lost their sheen from a financial or strategic perspective**

   One area where even the most capable business leaders frequently flounder is mapping an exit strategy. It can be tempting to remain committed to a clearly failing business in the hope that the tables will turn sometime in the future. It is also likely that exits can be misconstrued as succumbing to failure. But as the Tata Group has shown, through exits such as TOMCO and Tata DoCoMo (to Bharti), exiting when things are not looking good, is not a losing strategy. It can be the only wise route to avoid further damage and redeploy capital in more profitable ventures.

8. **Treat adversity as a productive challenge that can be overcome with grit and determination; the processes you have built over time get an opportunity to display their strength when adversity strikes**

   There has been no dearth of adverse situations in the history of the Tata Group. The several delays in approvals, attempts to curtail growth and potential reputational crises have plagued the business empire. The hold-up in the Tata-SIA venture is a good example of the bureaucratic and financial hurdles that the Tatas have suffered. It is important to remember that adversities strike the best of us, and remaining rooted and positive through them can make all the difference in the world.

9. **Think international in terms of standards, practices and markets, irrespective of the size of your business. Global practices have a way of boosting profitability and relevance over time**

   The Tata Group has consistently adopted global standards throughout its business. This has been a forward-thinking approach, well attuned to the global marketplace that doesn't have many of the barriers that existed in the past. So, for instance, the Tatas sought world-class fittings and designs for the Taj Hotel, handpicked by Mr Jamsetji

Tata. Mr J.R.D. Tata also ensured top-of-the-class service in Air India, personally flying in some of the flights and taking down notes. It is also what prompted international companies such as SIA to approach the Tatas to understand quality standards.

As of 2019, the Tata Group retains its stand as a conglomerate in the business world, continuing to thrive despite several episodes of turbulence in its history. However, the present business landscape is changing dramatically. The competition is cutthroat, and several players don't think twice about maligning each other's reputation. The Tata Group, too, has met with its fair share of challenges and setbacks. What is inspiring is how it has managed to emerge from them stronger than before.

In the years to come, it seems likely that the Tata Group will continue to partner in India's development story through strategic projects in core industries. It has been an enthralling journey that looks set to continue, constantly achieving newer peaks.

ANNEXURE 1

Tata Group's Select Acquisitions (2000–08)					
	Tata Company	*Acquired Company*	*Country*	*Stake Acquired*	*Value*
2000	Tata Tea	Tetley Group	United Kingdom	100%	$407 million
2004	Tata Motors	Daewoo Commercial Vehicle Company	South Korea	100%	$102 million
	Tata Communications	Tyco Global Network	United States	100%	$135 million
2005	Tata Steel	NatSteel Asia Pte. Ltd	Singapore	100%	$468.10 million
	Tata Motors	Hispano Carrocera	Spain	21% (balance bought in 2009)	€12 million
	Tata Chemicals	Indo Maroc Phosphore S.A.	Morocco	Equal partner	$38 million
	Indian Hotels	The Pierre	United States	Property lease	$45 million
	Tata Communications	Teleglobe International	Canada	100%	$239 million
	Tata Tea	Good Earth Corporation	United States	100%	$32 million
	Indian Hotels	Starwood Group (W Hotel)	Australia	100%	$29 million

2006	Tata Steel	Millennium Steel	Thailand	67.11%	$404 million
	Tata Coffee	Eight O'Clock Coffee Company	USA	100%	$220 million
2007	Tata Steel	Corus	United Kingdom	100%	$12.1 billion
	Indian Hotels	Campton Place Hotel	United States	100%	$58 million
	Tata Power	PT Kaltim Prima Coal and PT Arutmin	Indonesia	30% equity	$1.1 billion
2008	Tata Motors	Jaguar and Land Rover	United Kingdom	100%	$2.3 billion

ANNEXURE 2

CHAIRMEN OF THE TATA GROUP

Chairman	Tenure
Jamsetji Tata	1887–1904
Sir Dorabji Tata	1904–1932
Sir Nowrji Saklavata	1932–1939
J.R.D. Tata	1939–1991
Ratan Tata	1991–2012
Cyrus Mistry	2012–2016
Ratan Tata	2016–2017
Natarajan Chandrasekaran	2017–present

ANNEXURE 3

THE TATA TRUSTS

Year of Establishment	Trust	Role
1892	J.N. Tata Endowment Trust (Tata Educational Endowment Fund)	• Funds higher studies for students at leading global universities
1919	Sir Ratan Tata Trust	• Funds programmes and initiatives in education, health, rural livelihood, arts and culture
1932	Sir Dorabji Tata Memorial Trust	• Funds international cancer research in memory of Lady Meherbai, Sir Dorabji's wife, who died of leukaemia • Supports the Tata Institute of Social Sciences (1936); Tata Memorial Hospital (1941); Tata Institute of Fundamental Research (1945); the National Centre for the Performing Arts (1966); and Tata Medical Centre, Kolkata (2006)
1932	Lady Tata Memorial Trust, Lady Meherbai D. Tata Trust	• Funds the expenses for women pursuing social work and healthcare

1944	J.R.D. Tata Trust	• Supports overall development areas by running targeted programmes to achieve a better standard of living • Also provides the people of India with scholarships and grants
1974	Jamsetji Tata Memorial Trust	• Focuses on social welfare and health programmes
1974	Navajbai Ratan Tata Trust	• Works along with the Sir Ratan Tata Trust to bestow grants
2008	Tata Education and Development Trust	• Activities multifaceted in nature, promote social welfare